Shattered

S. Nelson

Shattered/ S.Nelson. -- 1st edition

ISBN-13: 978-1514347706
ISBN-10: 1514347709

This book is dedicated to one of the coolest women I've met along my new journey, Beth Miller. You've been one of my biggest cheerleaders, right from the beginning. Your love of my men is understandable, they are quite yummy. LOL. But your continued support is simply amazing. Thank you so much for always being there when I needed an extra pair of eyes to read over a scene I was struggling with. I love your enthusiasm for my work. I even love how you relentlessly tell me you don't need my stories edited in order to read them. You rock! And I'm only too happy to say I know you. You're a wonderful person and I look forward to many years of your love and craziness.

~1~

Sara

I once dreamed of a life where my happily ever after was waiting for me. Waiting for me to grab on with both hands and hold tight. All of the romance novels I'd ever read bragged such things, tempted me with a reality which simply didn't exist.

Not for me, at least.

My whole world had been turned upside-down in the blink of an eye. I racked my brain to try and figure out what I'd done to deserve Fate's cruel hand, but I'd come up blank.

I was a good person.

I didn't deserve to be thrown to the wolves.

Knowing there were many other people who had worse problems than me, I did my best to summon the strength needed to push through each and every day.

I was alive.

I was healthy.

I had good friends.

My dream of owning my own business came to fruition.

Those were the statements I repeated over and over to myself. My own positive mantra. But no matter how many times the words ran through my head, they never brought me any solace.

I did my absolute best to put on a strong front at work, not wanting Matt or Katherine to bombard me with questions. They both knew there was some sort of falling out between Alek and me, but thankfully, they were satisfied with the measly scraps I threw their way.

The explanation I gave was that we were simply not seeing each other anymore. I saw the look in Katherine's eyes when I'd told her. It was the 'I told you so' look but thankfully she never said the words out loud.

Matt, on the other hand, didn't believe me when I'd told him I was okay with not seeing Alek. The dead giveaway was when he placed his hand on my shoulder and squeezed, the compassionate look in his eyes undoing any resolve I'd been able to hold on to.

I bawled.

No holds barred.

Bawled.

Matt wrapped me in his warm embrace and told me he would *take care of* Alek. All I had to do was say the word. While I appreciated the gesture, I merely shook my head and tried my best to smile.

The one time Alek showed up at Full Bloom to try and talk to me was the only time I asked Matt to interfere. I couldn't bear to look at the man, let alone hear his voice.

I wasn't strong enough yet.

~~~~

An entire month passed since I last laid eyes on the man who devastated my entire world, ripping away any sense of security I was lucky enough to have built back up since moving to Seattle.

Falling for Alek Devera was a blessing and a curse. He'd made me trust in someone again, crushing the walls I'd built up to protect myself, making me feel alive again after so many years of simply drifting through life. He forced his way into my world, and I was powerless to stop him.

While he was a little over-the-top sometimes, his need to protect me made me feel wanted. He made me feel special. When I was attacked at Carlson's, he swooped in out of nowhere and rescued me from the drunk asshole who attacked me in the hallway. He insisted on having an alarm system installed in our apartment because he felt my safety was the number one priority. Hell, he even bought me a brand new car because he hated the thought of me being without a safe mode of transportation.

Safe. Safe. Safe.

I heard the word spewed from Alek's lips more times than I could remember.

Too bad he couldn't save me from my broken heart.

He'd called me so many times I lost count. When he couldn't get me on the phone, he tried Alexa. Thankfully, she never gave me the phone, although there were times the look on her face told me she wished I'd let him explain.

But I never did.

I wasn't ready to listen to what he had to say. Mainly because I didn't want to hear what I'd been thinking all along was the truth.

No. If I kept avoiding him, then there was a small chance he had a good explanation. What that was, I had no idea.

So I made sure to ignore any and all calls.

~2~

Sara

Stepping from the bathroom, I ran straight into Alexa coming down the hallway. I'd been crying. Again. She knew it as soon as she laid eyes onmy red, blotchy face. Trying to act as if nothing was wrong, I faintly smiled and continued on toward my room.

"Do you want to talk about it, Sara?" she asked as she followed behind me. I loved my best friend, but no amount of talking was going to heal me. I just needed to sleep. It was my new favorite escape.

"If you don't mind, I just want to go to bed. Maybe another time."

"You have to talk about it sometime, you know. You can't hole up here in your bedroom for the rest of your life." She sat on the edge of my mattress, her hand patting my leg in comfort.

"I know. Really, I do." I stared straight ahead. "I need more time."

"Well, I'll give you twenty-four more hours to put your head on straight," she said, her stern voice indicating how serious she was.

She caught my attention. "What do you mean?" I asked, shifting in uneasiness.

"Tomorrow night. You. Me. Girls' night. We're going out for a drink, and I won't take no for an answer." She stood and made to leave.

"Lex, please. I can't. Not yet." I didn't want to do it, but I had no more control. Tears broke free and coated my cheeks before I could even think to stop them.

"See? This is exactly why you fucking need to go out. Can't you see that?" *Why is she yelling at me?* "Stop feeling sorry for yourself, Sara. Get up, dust yourself off and move on with your life."

No one could say Alexa Bearnheart wasn't a great friend, but damn. Did she have to go all tough love on my ass?

"Fine," I mumbled, a small smile finding its way onto my otherwise sad face. I loved feisty Alexa, even if I was her latest victim.

"Yay!" she cheered, dancing her way out of my room.

For the love. What did I just agree to?

~~~~

For as busy as the shop was, the clock didn't seem to move. The stale moments of time were laughing at me, baiting me with their callous disregard for my need to end the day.

Alexa and I had agreed to meet at a neighborhood bar after I closed up for the evening. I was trying my best to remain positive, knowing full well I deserved a small reprieve from my tortured heart, even if that pardon came in the form of alcohol.

Hell, my best friend deserved it for putting up with me the past month, all mopey and moody.

I arrived at precisely six o'clock and stood outside to wait for her, trying my best to tamp down the incessant need to run home and jump under the covers.

Nervously shifting from one foot to the other, I counted the minutes until my best friend arrived. She was usually on time, so I expected her to pull up any second. But after more time passed of no Alexa, I grabbed my phone, preparing to call and find out what was holding her up. As I was about to connect the call, I had an uneasy feeling someone was standing behind me.

A little too close for comfort.

The hairs on the back of my neck bristled, my body suddenly becoming warm even though the night's chilly air did its best to bind me in a cool embrace.

Without turning around, I knew exactly who it was.

No amount of time could erase the effect he had on me when he was near.

It was as if there was an imaginary electrical current passing between us whenever we shared the same space.

Spinning around slowly, I chose to keep my eyes closed longer than normal. The more seconds which passed where he didn't infiltrate my world, the better. I knew I was being ridiculous, but it worked for me.

I eventually opened my eyes and there he was, standing not two feet away from me.

Dressed in one of his designer suits, he should have looked impeccable, but instead, he appeared disheveled. His hair was behaving in the unruly way which made him look sexier, even if I hadn't wanted to notice as much. But it was his face which displayed all the hurt and agony he was going through. Still the most handsome man I'd ever seen, he looked beat down. And ragged. There were dark circles splayed underneath his eyes, no doubt from lack of sleep. His posture was one of defeat, portraying a heartbroken man to anyone who cared to pay attention. *I* noticed, simply because I shared the same affliction.

Was it merely a coincidence Alek had been waiting outside the same bar where Alexa and I had agreed to meet? Had she set the whole thing up? Had they been in contact with one another? If so, how often had they been talking behind my back? Too many questions raced through my mind, but there were no answers. None which would have calmed me down, at least. I was beyond upset. I knew she was only trying to do what she thought she should, but it didn't stop me from being pissed at her. We would surely be having words as soon as I arrived home.

Seeing him again brought everything back to the forefront.

The lying.

The betrayal.

The heartache.

Realizing being so close to one another wasn't a good idea, I turned away and walked briskly back toward my car.

His car.

Whatever.

I'd only agreed to keep his extravagant gift until I purchased my own, but since we weren't together anymore, I wanted to give it back immediately. I tried, numerous times, making Alexa follow me to his house to drop it off in front of his gate, but he kept returning it. So I gave up until I found a way for him to keep it for good.

I didn't make it far before he was right on my heels. "Sara, please stop. I need to explain myself. Please, just give me a chance," he pleaded, reaching out and gripping my elbow. His hold threw me off-balance, allowing him to whip me around so we were face to face again.

Our whole situation quickly replayed in my head, from how I felt when I was with him, to our lustful nights together, to the discovery of his secret. So many emotions plagued me. But unfortunately, none of them were going to save me from what I was about to do.

Or should I say...save him from what was about to happen.

Before my brain could shut down the impulse, a quick rush of air broke the silence between us as my palm connected with his cheek.

I wanted him to hurt the same way I did.

My hand instantly started to throb. Surprisingly, he stumbled back a step, actually having the decency to look ashamed. "I deserved that," he muttered. He kept his eyes locked on me, waiting for something. Anything. Waiting for me to speak, or maybe waiting for me to strike him again.

I did neither.

We stood there for what felt like an eternity, eyes locked on one another. I couldn't help the sappy emotion which chose to take hold. I missed him. Missed looking at his face which I loved so much. Missed his smell and the feel of being held in his arms. I missed talking to him and sharing stories. Hell, I even missed arguing with him.

But no amount of missing could obliterate the feeling of hopelessness which wrapped around me. And if I didn't do something about it soon, it would swallow me up and never let me go.

He was the first to break the uncomfortable silence. "Can we go somewhere more private so I can fully explain myself?" His dejected gaze pleaded with me to give him the chance he needed, but I couldn't do it. Not right then.

"I can't," I said softly. I wanted to yell and scream at him, but what good would it do? "I don't have anything to say to you, Alek, and quite honestly, I don't care to hear what you have to tell me." I looked down at my shoes. "I need more time."

If Alek had been a sensitive man, I would have thought our situation was weakening him. His eyes were glassy and red, indicating he was going to cry. But that wasn't him. He was strong and unwavering, passionate and dominant. Yes, there were glimpses of sensitivity I'd seen during our time together, but it was mostly during the intimate times we'd shared. The far-off look which would take over his features as if his feelings toward me were too much for him.

But I knew he was only doing his best to not get caught. What I'd thought were genuine feelings for me were simply disguises for the secrets he held close.

He sucked in a ragged breath and straightened his spine. "How much time? I can't bear to be separated from you." He never broke eye contact, pulling me in with his steadfast gaze. "You have to believe I was only looking out for you, trying to keep you safe. I swear it." He advanced toward me, reaching out to try and touch me. I backed away. When he saw I was ready to leave again, he uttered the words I'd only dreamed about. "I love you, Sara. I love you so much I can't breathe without you. I would never, ever, do anything to hurt you. Please..."

Feeling as if someone had gut-punched me, I stumbled backward, thankfully catching myself before I hit the pavement. Why did he have to tell me he loved me for the first time under these circumstances? Why couldn't he have gifted me with his words after a night of making love? Or just during any of our other encounters? I would have even accepted them during one of our heated arguments. But not there, not like that. I found I was still affected by them but not as much as I would have liked to have been, due to our unraveling relationship.

"If you loved me so much, you should have been honest with me about whatever was going on right from the beginning." Realizing I couldn't torture myself any longer, I turned back around and continued on toward my car, trying to escape the hurt emanating from every pore of his body.

Thankfully, he didn't try to stop me.

~3~

Sara

"How many times have you talked to him, Alexa?" I shouted, unable to control the rising octave of my voice. I tried to coax myself down from the ledge the whole time I drove home, doing my best to convince myself my best friend did what she thought she should. But the fact of the matter was...she betrayed me. She handed me off to the wolf with no regard for my emotional safety.

Since I had no idea who Alek really was, she also put me in physical danger. Who the hell knew what he would have done to me, given the right, or wrong, circumstance. In reality, did I think he would ever harm me? No. But I'd been wrong about him so far, so I couldn't trust my own intuition when it came to him.

Thankfully, nothing happened from our little surprise encounter, other than him getting smacked, of course. While it should have made me feel good to lash out at him, it made me feel worse. He had reduced me to someone who I didn't recognize. I wasn't that person. I didn't purposely hurt people, emotionally *or* physically.

But when I was around him, all sense of my true self flew right out the window.

With my hands on my hips, I crowded Alexa's personal space. Advancing a single step in her direction caused her to fall down on the couch. She looked up at me with regret and sadness in her eyes. She knew she fucked up, but I still wasn't going to let her off the hook too easily.

"How. Many. Times?" I repeated.

I'd never seen Alexa Bearnheart back down from anyone before, but she knew enough about my state of mind to not mess with me. She was playing the role she should, of a friend who did me wrong.

Looking down at her lap, she answered. "Only a few times." When she heard me gasp, she snapped her head up to look at me. "I swear, Sara. I never meant to go behind your back. It's just..."

"Just what?"

A long sigh fell from her lips. "He sounded so lost. His voice cracked when he was begging me to put you on the phone. I swear to Christ, Sara, he sounded like he was going to cry, and although it shouldn't have, it broke my heart."

Alexa reached out to snag my hand in hers, but I moved away. I loved my friend, but right then I would end up smacking her if she touched me.

So many emotions dueled inside me. It was as if I wasn't even in my own body, the feelings I was experiencing so foreign to me. I wasn't even over the feelings Alek evoked from me and there I was, dealing with Alexa's betrayal. Maybe I was overreacting a little, but I didn't care. She had to know how much she hurt me.

The last thing I wanted was to feel as if I couldn't confide in her. I had to know that what I told her would be kept between us. That she had my back, no matter what.

"Your loyalty is to me, Alexa. Not him. What you did was wrong." I took a seat next to her on the couch, still keeping a safe distance. "I know you think you were only trying to help me. But you have to let me deal with this on my own terms, in my own way. Only *I* will know when the time is right to hear what he has to say." My anger slowly waned, the look on her face making me want to comfort her. But I didn't. She had to know I was serious.

"I'm so sorry. I swear I'll never talk to him again." Her nervousness had her biting her nails, a habit she had tried to break over and over again. "I merely thought if I could arrange for you two to meet, to talk, you would resolve this issue and get back together. I mean, come on, Sara. If there's no hope for the two of you, then what chance do *I* have?" She attempted to smile but faltered, her grin never truly reaching her eyes.

"Alexa, I have no idea why he has all those freaking pictures of me. For all we know, he could be some kind of crazy, psycho stalker."

"You know, deep down, he's not. Although, he's not making a good case for himself right now. I get it. But you won't know until you give him a chance to explain." She moved closer and grabbed my hand. I let her. "I love you. I only want what's best for you. I thought if you would hear him out and give him another chance, you could get the hell out of this funk you have yourself in." Squeezing my palm in hers, she said, "But I've learned my lesson. Trust me. I won't interfere again. Do you forgive me?" she asked, looking hopeful I would say yes.

"I suppose." I shrugged. "But if you go back on your word and talk to him behind my back...I won't forgive you again."

"I promise. No more. I won't even say his name."

"Good," I said, desperate to change the subject.

After we were done talking about the latest gossip at her job, I decided what I needed was a nice, long, hot shower.

The spray of the water did nothing but wash away a tiny amount of tension from my body. Did I really think a hot escape would do the trick? Maybe. A little.

I should know better than to hope for such things.

As my head hit the pillow and my eyes became heavy, I prayed for my dreams to give me some reprieve. Ever since I ran away from Alek, my nightmares had come back in full force.

Or should I say memories?

I didn't want to do it. I willed my mind to go somewhere else, but it didn't listen. As I drifted off into an uneasy sleep, the recollections of long ago rushed forward with a vengeance, wrapping their harsh, ugly hands around my soul and squeezed until I'd given in.

For the first time in almost eight years, I'd let myself drift back to the day I was taken.

~4~

Sara

"Are you almost ready, dear?" Gram yells from the bottom of the stairs. Rushing around and getting ready for my job at the bookstore is a normal occurrence for me. Since I don't have enough money saved for my own car yet, I have to rely on my grandmother for rides to and from work. I hate putting her out like this, but I don't have another choice right now. When I can, I'll catch a ride with the girls I work with, but it isn't often at all.

"Yeah, I'll be right down."

Grabbing my name tag from the dresser, I hurry down the stairs so fast I almost run smack-dab right in to her. She's waiting for me at the bottom, and my clumsiness almost surely caused a detour to the hospital.

Laughing, she grabs my arms to steady me, looks me deep in the eyes and smiles.

I'm instantly put at ease.

I'm so grateful for every day my grandma Rose is in my life. She really is my second mother. I don't know what type of person I would have turned out to be if it wasn't for her stepping in and taking care of me after my mother died.

Thankfully, the bookstore is only a ten-minute ride from our house. When we finally pull up front, I hop out, but only after giving her a big kiss and telling her I love her.

Having five minutes to spare, I race toward the break room and throw my purse in my locker. I prepare for my shift, taking a quick drink before heading out to the floor to deal with the customers.

It's relatively busy for a Wednesday evening, which is just fine with me. Time always goes by quicker when I'm busy.

"Hey, Sara, there you are. Can you help me stock the new shipment of books? I have to rearrange this display over here and replace them with the ones that just came in. Then we have to move the initial display over there in the far right-hand corner." I don't even see Karen come up behind me. But it doesn't stop her from continuing on, not even giving me a second thought as to why I nearly jumped ten feet in the air.

"Sure. Show me what you need me to do," I say as I get down to business. "Oh, by the way, do you think you can possibly give me a ride home after work tonight? You're working until close, right?"

"Yeah, I am, and of course I can. No problem."

We make quick work of dismantling the display and replace it with the new one. Once we're done with our project, we fall right into our other duties, such as taking inventory and assisting customers.

On break, I call my gram and tell her I have a ride home so she doesn't have to come and pick me up. The weather had turned and rain pelted the ground outside, making me more grateful to Karen since I hated dragging my gram out in this type of weather.

I'm busy cleaning up a stack of books someone knocked over when she comes running over. "Hey, Sara! Look who it is," she whispers, rudely pointing at someone. "I can't believe they still let him work here. He's super weird." She leans in close for her next statement. "I don't know why you even bother to engage him in conversation." She's not-so-subtly referring to Samuel, the maintenance guy who works here.

He's busy fixing a busted light fixture, glancing over in our direction, smiling when he sees I'm looking at him. Then his eyes fall on Karen and he looks away quickly. "Oh, how can you stand it? Doesn't he creep you out?"

"Karen, stop being so mean. He never did anything to anyone."

"Not who lived to tell about it, anyway. Just be careful around him, Sara." I let out a restrained sigh as she walks away to help a customer.

Samuel started working at the bookstore about eight months ago. Being the nephew of the owner seems to work against the poor guy. I hear what people say, that no one else would ever hire him, that he's *too strange to work anywhere else, that it isn't fair they have to share the same space with him.*

While I do my best not to judge him, I can see where people might think certain things about him, his appearance sometimes adding to the situation. He's tall and more on the lanky side, wearing clothes ill-fitting for his form. Shaggy hair and sporadic facial hair are a norm for him. Simply because he doesn't fit into society's version of what's normal shouldn't automatically cause people to shun him, should it?

People are mean. Yes, he's different. But no, he's never said a mean word to anyone, nor has he ever done anything questionable, either. Not that I've seen, at least.

My boss explained he is emotionally stunted for his age of thirty-five. He's well enough to live on his own, but he doesn't adapt too well to normal social interactions. Every time I cross paths with him, he smiles and continues on with whatever project he's working on.

The more time passed, the less nervous I became. We exchange simple niceties every now and then, talking about the weather or how I was doing in school.

Karen teases me. All the time. She says he has a crush on me and I should watch out before he ends up wearing my skin as a suit someday. I don't laugh because I don't want to encourage her.

Someone has to stick up for him, right?

I truly feel bad for him. I'm sure he hears her ramblings, mainly because she isn't quiet when she's talking about him. Sometimes I catch his eye and witness the sadness there. But I smile, trying to reassure him not everyone is like her.

Coming out of the ladies room, I run right into him on accident. "Oh, excuse me, Samuel. Sorry, I didn't see you there."

"No...no...it's my fault. I shouldn't have been standing so close to the door. I shouldn't have been so close," he repeats, flustered and shaking his head back and forth. He continues to mumble as he stands close to me.

Some days, he's okay and some days, the smallest things seem to upset him, which cause him to apologize profusely, becoming upset with himself.

I reach out and touch his forearm, trying my best to calm him down. "Don't worry about it. Seriously, Samuel, it was merely an accident."

My touch seems to do the trick. He instantly relaxes. "Okay, Sara," he says as he looks at the ground. "I have to go now...I have to fix the sink in the men's room." He walks away, his eyes still fixated on the ground.

I'm on break a little while later when Karen comes into the back of the store. "Sorry, Sara, but something came up and I can't give you a ride home after all. Your gram can come pick you up, though, right?"

"Yeah, don't worry about it. Thanks anyway." I don't want to bring her out in this weather, but it looks like I have no other choice.

Samuel walks in on the end of our conversation and must notice my slight distress at the news.

"I can give you a ride home," he offers as he looks at me across the room. He's standing there with a hopeless expression on his face, no doubt still recovering from his small episode earlier.

"No, it's okay. I wouldn't want to put you out. But thank you, I appreciate it."

"I really don't mind at all. Didn't you say you lived kind of close to here? It's no big deal."

I quickly think about this. I'm not one hundred percent sure about it, but at the same time I'm concerned about making my gram drive in this weather to pick me up.

In the end, her safety wins out over my quick reservation.

"Okay, but only if you are sure." He nods.

We exchange a small smile before I pass him on my way back out to the sales floor.

It's finally time to leave. I follow Samuel out to his truck, ignoring the whispers of my co-workers.

Strapping in, I give him my address as he makes a right out of the parking lot. There is an uncomfortable silence between us. Am I simply nervous because I've only interacted with him at work? Or is there something else brewing inside? An unnerving instinct trying to warn me of something?

Pushing my erratic thoughts aside, I stare out the window.

He manages to scare me when he speaks, silence otherwise surrounding us. "I'm so happy you've finally agreed to be with me."

The rain hitting the windshield muffles what he says. He didn't say what I thought he did, did he?

"Excuse me?" *I say, praying the next words out of his mouth are something which won't freak me out.*

"I've waited a long time for this, Sara," *he declares as he turns his head to look at me.* "The first time I saw you, I knew we had a special connection." *A far-off look invades his pupils, driving home how far off-kilter he's becoming.*

My reality is certainly not the same as his.

Frantically thinking of something to say, I start to shift in my seat, nervousness taking over with each pass of the road.

"Samuel," *I start cautiously,* "I need you to pull over and let me out, please. I'll call for another ride home."

His hands grip the steering wheel so tight his knuckles lose all color. "Why do you want to leave me already?"

How do I even respond to such a question? Because you're freaking me the fuck out *is probably not the right thing to say right now, although it's the honest-to-God truth.*

"Why, Sara?" *he shouts, pounding his fist against the leather wheel. I physically jump, moving closer to my door. This is going from bad to worse. Fast.*

"*I need to go home. Please. Please, just take me home,*" I beg.

Without missing a beat, he answers me and the chills wrap around my spine and squeeze. I almost lose my lunch all over the front seat.

"*I* am *taking you home,*" he declares. "*Our home.*"

My heart plummets.

My breathing becomes erratic.

My tears spill forth, washing away any hope of escape.

Running my hands up and down my thighs I realize my phone is in my purse. By my feet. All I have to do is lean down and grab it. As I move forward, Samuel turns his head in my direction, watching me as much as he can without crashing his vehicle.

"*What are you doing?*"

"*Nothing,*" I whisper, sitting back in my seat. Samuel is proving to be unpredictable, and I'm not sure what I should do. He's showing me a side of himself I thought only existed in other people's imaginations. And because of my need to prove them wrong, I ended up in his clutches.

Exactly where he wanted me.

Every time I smiled in his direction, trying to appease his nervousness, he took my niceness as an indication of my feelings for him. Or what he thought were my feelings. I was simply trying to not judge, not treat him like everyone else did. I knew he was different, and I wasn't going to be like everyone else.

I should have been.

I should have never made eye contact.

I should have never been nice.

I would have been safe.

If I don't do or say anything right now, if I let him drive me closer to wherever it is he's taking me, then I will lose.

My freedom.

My happy little bubble.

My world.

To hell with it! *I dive forward and retrieve my cell as quickly as I can. Grabbing my only hope, I swipe the screen and do my best to dial 911. I know in my gut I won't complete the call. But I try anyway.*

My sudden movements cause Samuel to whip the wheel to the right and skid to a stop on the side of the highway, kicking up gravel all around us.

I reach for the handle to jump out of his truck, but he grabs my arm before I can escape.

"No!" he shouts. "Why are you being like this, Sara? Why are you trying to leave me?"

I have no words for him. I don't even fully comprehend what's taking place right now. I know I'm in danger, but it's like I'm moving in slow motion, an alternate world dancing around me. Pulling me in deeper and deeper until I can't even hear him.

I see him, though.

He's angry.

So angry.

The muscles in his face start to tick, tiny spasms jumping the more upset he becomes. His eyes blink in quick succession, his hold on me tightening the more his body betrays him.

"I...I...just want to go...go," I stammer. "Please, let me out." I try to shrug free, but it's no use.

I'm not going anywhere.

Glancing into his eyes, I see my future and it terrifies me. I bear witness to the man sitting next to me come unhinged. My life isn't my own anymore, of this I'm sure. Lost in my own dread, I don't even see it coming.

A sharp pain to my temple throws me into unconsciousness.

~~~~

The world starts to fade in and out as a ripping pain tears through my brain. I try to reach up to grab my head, but I can't. My arms are restrained, a coarse rope grating against my sensitive skin. I make it worse with each struggled attempt.

I try to remember how I ended up here and that's when the memories come flooding in, fitting all the jagged pieces of the puzzle together.

I can't believe I thought he was harmless. It was so obvious to everyone else around me, but for some unexplainable reason, I chose to turn a blind eye to what was staring me right in the face.

I don't want to be the type of person who judges others simply because they're different. In this instance, though, I should have followed the flock.

A faint sound above tears me from my thoughts, instantly making my heart beat faster. The floorboards creak with each step, the sound eerily reminding me of a horror film. Shrouded in darkness, I can't see a thing. But I can hear. The sound becomes more prominent, getting closer until I hear a door open. Someone descends the rickety stairs, and I can only assume it's the man who now holds me captive.

A faint light is turned on in the farthest part of the room. Even though it isn't bright, it takes me some time to fully adjust to it. When I turn my head, I can see the back of Samuel. He's fiddling with something, but I'm not quite sure what. He's blocking my view.

"Samuel," I call out. "Where am I?" I'm hoping if I talk to him, engage him in conversation, he'll see what he's doing is wrong. There has to be a rational man inside him somewhere, and I'm going to do my best to find him.

He doesn't answer, but he stops moving.

"*Samuel? Please, look at me.*" *My voice is a liar. I sound calm, but I'm anything but. I'm terrified and cracking on the inside.*

"*Sara. Oh, Sara. I never meant for this to happen. You have to believe me. But you made me so angry. Why did you try to leave me?*" *He's starting to become anxious and twitchy the more he speaks.*

"*I'm sorry. I just wanted to go home to see my gram. I didn't mean to upset you.*" *I expel a deep breath before adding,* "*Can you let me go now? We can pretend none of this happened.*" *A tear escapes and dances down my cheek.* "*I won't tell anyone. I promise.*"

He quickly turns around and walks in my direction, an object held loosely in his hands. I try to see what it is, but I don't have a good angle.

"*I can't, Sara. I'm so sorry, but I can't. You'll tell, and I can't go back there. I have such nightmares, and no one helps me.*" *His voice trails off.* "*No one helps me,*" *he repeats.*

"*I won't tell, Samuel. I promise. Please, untie me. No one will ever know. I'll tell my gram I stopped off to do some shopping before coming home. She'll believe me. Please...just let me go home. Please, Samuel,*" *I plead.*

He hovers over me, his hands hiding behind his back. "*I'm sorry, Sara. I can't.*" *He moves a smelly rag over my mouth and nose in one quick motion. I try to fight and catch my breath, but I only make it worse. I quickly fade back into unconsciousness, blackness creeping in all around to swallow me up.*

Time passes undetected, consciousness a fleeting luxury. I'm losing the ability to think straight, to wrap my head around the severity of my demise.

It's like I'm in a constant state of fuzziness.

During one of my brief moments of alertness, I overhear Samuel talking to someone at his front door. I try to struggle against my restraints, but it's no use. Moments later, I hear him walk across the room above me, round the corner and start his descent to my dark dungeon.

"Who was at the door, Samuel? Was it someone looking for me? Please, Samuel...please, just let me go. I swear I won't tell anyone." *I tell him over and over I won't give him away, but he never believes me.*

"I can't do that, Sara. You belong here with me now. If we're going to make this relationship work, you're going to have to trust me." *He utters his words with calmness, but there is an undeniable annoyance laced behind each syllable.*

Relationship? What the hell is he talking about? *He's even more delusional than I had originally thought.*

Knowing better than to antagonize him by rebutting his earlier statement, I simply ask him again who was at the door, doing so in the calmest tone I can muster. "Samuel, can you please tell me who you were talking to?"

"*A detective.*" *He doesn't offer up any more information. I'm hopeful to hear they're at least looking for me, not realizing how long I've actually been missing.*

"*Can you tell me how long I've been here?*" *When he doesn't answer right away, I continue interrogating him.* "*Samuel?*'

"*What?*" *he angrily shouts at me.*

I have to tread carefully because I don't know what he's fully capable of, not wanting his anger to escalate and fatally harm me.

"*Would you be able to please tell me how long I have been here with you?*"

"*Four days,*" *he says before turning off the light and disappearing up the steps.*

Left in darkness once again, I have nothing but time to think. My poor grandmother is probably going out of her mind with worry. She knows I would never take off, so she has to realize I'm in some sort of danger. But what's the hold-up? I know people saw me hop into his truck, so why aren't they busting down the door to rescue me?

I drift off to sleep, my weariness too much to keep me alert any longer.

Sometimes, I feel his fingers work their way through my hair, relishing the feel of me. Other times, I feel his face directly above mine, almost touching me.

He feeds me very little, no doubt making sure I remain weak. Each time I need to go to the bathroom, I have to wait until he decides to come and check on me. Even then, he has me use a bedpan. It's humiliating to say the least, but I have to focus on the bigger picture.

I'm still alive, so there's hope, albeit faint, but hope nonetheless.

The next time he wakes me up, I decide to try something different with him.

"Samuel, if we're going to make our relationship work, you're going to have to trust me enough to untie me." Please...please, let this work.

"I don't believe you, Sara. You don't want to stay. You want to leave me...just like everyone else."

"No, I don't, I swear it. I want to be here with you, I promise I do. You have to believe me."

"Stop it! Stop lying to me, Sara!" he shouts. Not sure how far he'll go, I fall silent. "I'll be down later with some soup for dinner."

Startled awake by a loud noise, I try to focus on what I think I hear. Voices. Coming from directly above me. Maybe I've finally fallen off the edge of sanity.

Am I hallucinating?

The voice proceeds to become louder with each passing second. Someone is shouting. Then, as if all of my prayers are answered, I hear actual words.

"Where is she, Samuel? Just tell us where she is and everything will be all right." I don't hear my captor respond.

After what seems like forever, I hear loud, heavy footsteps pounding down the wooden steps. I pray it isn't Samuel. I pray it's anyone else.

"Down here! She's down here!" I hear a man shout. These are the last words I make out before slipping back into the darkness

~ ~ ~ ~

Samuel Colden held me hostage for nine long, torturous days. The detectives told me he had formed an unhealthy attachment, believing we were indeed involved in a relationship. He had somehow gotten hold of my work ID badge and made hundreds of copies, plastering them all over his house. He even taped images of himself next to them.

A happy couple.

A farce to feed his delirium.

He continued to go to work during the days I was trapped inside his house, pretending as if everything was completely normal. I'd found out later on people had asked about me, wondering why I never showed up for my shifts. It wasn't until they called my house two days later that they found out I was even missing.

Even though there were witnesses placing me with Samuel the night I disappeared, it still took them nine days to come and rescue me. But I was grateful they found me at all.

Thankfully, he didn't sexually assault me. While he'd torn away all sense of safety and security, at least he hadn't stolen my innocence. The only comfort I had was the fact he was taken away and would be locked up for a very, very long time.

So began my journey to overcome my tragedy. I worked hard to not let it define me.

Everything was going well until Alek shattered my world.

~5~

Alek

I'd let another two weeks go by without contacting Sara. She said she needed more time and I gave it to her, even when it killed me to do so. Not being near her was tearing me apart, a little bit every single day.

Ever since I stepped through the door of Full Bloom, my world had been altered forever.

For the better.

Seeing the effect I had on her was mind-blowing, the best-case scenario I could have hoped for. But I never thought I would be caught up in her just as much. Looking back, I didn't know why I'd been surprised. She was beautiful and intelligent, someone who wasn't afraid to tell me what she thought. A trait I didn't even know I'd been longing for in a woman.

I loved the back and forth between us. Me trying to exert my need to be in control and her pushing back at every turn.

She was a challenge.

She was a breath of fresh air.

Knowing full well I shouldn't have expressed my feelings for her the way I did, I simply couldn't help myself.

I love Sara Hawthorne.

With all my heart.

From the outside, it might look like I rushed in too fast, blinders on, letting my emotions rule me. But no one had any idea what had been going on for years.

Yes, I'd officially met Sara barely five months before, but I'd been keeping an eye on her for the past eight years.

And it was finally time I told her the whole sordid story.

~~~~

Waiting outside her shop was killing me. I knew it was going to be difficult to convince her to speak to me, but I was certainly up for the challenge.

I didn't have a choice.

It was time she heard me out, listened to my side of the story. I knew she probably thought I was some sort of deranged stalker, but it couldn't be further from the truth.

I'd been enlisted to protect her, her safety always being my concern. Even present day.

I saw the instant she made her way outside, locking the door behind her, unaware I was watching her. But then again, she'd always been unaware. It was for her own good. I couldn't even imagine how difficult she would have been had she known she'd had a shadow.

Opening the back door of the sedan, I stepped out and cautiously approached her. Her back was still turned toward me, allowing me a few precious seconds to muster up the strength needed to deal with everything.

With the final turn of the shop's lock, she pivoted on her heel and came face to face with me, the look of shock on her face making me want to reach out and assure her.

I'd given her the space she needed, but it was time she gave me what I wanted. *No, what I need.*

I approached her cautiously, especially since the last time I was close she lashed out and smacked me across the face. While it hurt like a bitch, I knew I deserved every bit of her anger, both physical and emotional.

I knew she wanted to hurt me as much as I'd hurt her.

"Alek, stop right there. I don't have anything to say to you, so don't waste your breath," she said, frustrated, knowing I wasn't going to leave her alone so soon. "Go home, Alek...just go home."

"You have to talk to me sometime, Sara. You have to let me explain. You'll understand everything once you give me a chance." I locked eyes on her, silently pleading with her to give in.

I was tired and worn down. Never in a million years did I ever think I'd let a woman affect me in such a way, weaving her essence into every cell in my body.

Ever trying to appear unaffected, I knew she saw me falter, if even for a little bit.

"I don't *have* to do anything, Alek. I need more time." She turned away and started walking toward her car. I wanted to yell at her, try and make her see she was being unreasonable, but I'd for sure lock up all her defenses. No, I had to handle it the only way I knew how.

Hurrying my steps, I made my way in front of her retreating body, blocking her route to escape.

"I don't have any more time for this shit, Sara," I proclaimed before I picked her up and flung her over my shoulder. Her scent instantly filled my nose, memories of being buried deep inside her too strong to push aside. I was instantly hard, a happening which was more of an annoyance than anything. Mainly because there wasn't a damn thing I could do about it.

She fought me like I knew she would, but I wasn't letting her walk away again. A few paces were all it took for me to arrive at the back door of the car. I'd chosen to bring my driver along. There was no way I was going to drive while she tried her best to escape from me, endangering us both.

"Put me down!" she screamed. I was sure we were quite the sight, but thankfully no one approached me, sheer determination written all over my face. Anyone could see if they'd looked close enough.

Her small fists pounded against my back, but I never flinched. My only goal was to get her alone and make her listen to me. I knew once she heard my explanation, we could start over, right where we left off.

At least I was hoping as much.

Opening the door, I gently shoved her into the backseat—if that was even possible, to gently shove. Or maybe I intently shoved her inside. No matter. She was in my car and my plan was working.

Knowing what she'd do, I'd been prepared for her every action. I had her on her back before she reached for the opposite door handle, slamming my own door and yelling to the driver to take off. He didn't even bat an eyelash, pulling out into traffic as if this was an everyday occurrence for me.

Which it wasn't. Thank God. Although, who the hell knew what the future held. I could fully envision having to throw Sara over my shoulder. For her insolence. For her safety. Hell, just for fun.

We were nose to nose, our lips almost touching. I'd wanted nothing more than to attack her mouth, but I wouldn't take it there.

Yet.

When our breathing was the only sound in the car, she spoke and broke the silence. "You're crushing me, Alek," she mumbled, my weight obviously cutting off her air supply. I'd been so lost in her I hadn't even realized I was still lying on top of her.

"If I let you up, are you going to behave?" I asked, knowing full well she wanted nothing more than to tell me to fuck off.

She never answered my question. Instead, she grit her teeth and said, "Get off me."

"Fine," I replied. I had nothing else to say.

The drive back to my house was uneventful, which was both good and bad. Good, because she wasn't fighting me anymore, never even questioning where I was taking her. Bad, *because* she didn't put up a fight. I'd hope I hadn't lost her. Not yet.

Once we arrived, I opened my door, reaching for her hand behind me as I exited the vehicle. She batted it away, instead moving further into the car. Holding the door open, I waited her out. Finally, she made her exit, huffing as she walked past me, brushing my shoulder with hers. The slight touch already making my body come alive.

I smiled. *At least she didn't run down the driveway and try to hop the gate.*

Folding her arms, she sighed loudly as I approached, fumbling for my keys. She rolled her eyes when I looked at her, making my dick twitch in my pants. Again.

"Do you want something to drink?" I offered as I allowed her to walk inside ahead of me.

"No," she answered. Short and to the point. "So, where do you want to do this? Here?" she asked, pointing toward the sitting room. Not waiting for my response, she brushed past me, her shoulder touching mine again, as she stepped into the large open space.

I wanted to tell her I'd much rather talk in my bedroom. Naked. But I didn't think that'd fly too well with her. *One step at a time.*

"Yes. But I'm going to need a drink, so give me a second."

"I'm sure you *are* going to need it, so feel free."

I smiled as I turned my back toward her, not wanting to upset her further, having her thinking this was all a joke. I knew exactly how serious this was. I was smirking because I loved her sass. Most of the time.

Pouring myself a decent-size drink, I gulped down half, summoning all the courage and patience I needed for our talk.

Expelling a deep breath, I closed my eyes and counted to five. Most people count till ten, but I couldn't wait that long. I needed to start so we could get back to where we left off.

Her naked, underneath me.

Turning around, I took a few steps until I was near her, lowering myself so I was sitting on the far end of the couch. I didn't want to crowd her, needing her to be as open to my explanation as possible.

I parted my lips to start but she cut me off, spewing out questions faster than I could comprehend the words.

"Did you think I would casually ask you why you had stalker-ish photos of me, Alek? Did you want me to wait around for the answer, not knowing whether you were a danger to me in some way? You're always going on and on about my safety. Well, do you think it's safe for me to be in the presence of someone who's hiding a secret from me?"

Holy shit! Talk about diving right into it. I ran my hand through my hair, clenching the back of it in frustration. She wasn't going to make this easy on me. Not one little bit.

"I know why you were upset—" I offered, but she cut me off again before I could finish.

"AM! Why I *am* upset, not *were* upset!" she yelled, finally letting go of her calm demeanor. The anger danced behind her eyes, showing me her frustration grew the longer we sat there together.

I had to do something and fast.

Inching closer to her on the couch, I put my hand on her thigh, her dress riding up and revealing some of her lovely skin. Touching her sent a jolt through me, making my heart pick up the pace. But just like in the car, she batted my hand away.

For a brief moment, we sat there and studied one another. I wasn't sure if she was going to bolt, and I was sure she didn't know what was going to come flying from my mouth.

"Where do I even start, baby?" I whispered, still holding our firm eye contact.

"Don't call me that, Alek. You forfeited your right to call me such things."

My face fell. What she'd said wasn't exactly a surprise, but it hurt nonetheless.

"I'll start from the beginning, from when I first saw you." Her face took on an expression of relief mixed with reservation. I didn't blame her.

She looked away from me and shifted in her seat, tucking her long hair behind her ear before turning her stare back onto me.

I drew a deep breath and continued. "It was about eight years ago when I first laid eyes on you. Well, to be exact, it was a picture of you.

"Where did you see—?"

"Sara, I'm asking for you to please allow me to tell you the whole story, from start to finish. Then you can ask me as many questions as you like. But please...let me get through this. It's hard for me, and I don't want you to be any more upset with me than you already are. Although, I know I can't control what you feel, I can at least give you all the facts and prove to you I was only ever looking out for you."

"Fine." She sighed, motioning for me to start talking again.

"As I was saying, the first time I saw you was in a picture—your high school picture, to be exact. You see, my grandfather was away on business when he'd taken ill. I'd dropped everything and flew right out to visit him. He had checked into a local hospital, not wanting to risk his health further by flying back home first. It was a smart decision on his part because as it turned out, he had a bad case of pneumonia. They kept him for almost two weeks. At Belford Memorial Hospital. In Florida."

I waited for something to dawn on her. Some part of my story should've been familiar. Maybe she was too wrapped up in my tale to recognize it. But before I spoke again, it was there, recognition lighting her eyes like a fire in the night. Her mouth fell open and her breath quickened.

"Belford Memorial? That was the name of the hospital my grandmother was in. She was there because of a hip replacement." Her lips snapped shut immediately after offering the information.

I continued. "When I walked into the hospital to visit him, they told me he'd been moved. To Room 312." Again, I stopped and waited for her to catch on.

"Room 312?" she whispered, her hand slightly covering her mouth in disbelief.

"Yes. Well, actually he was in Room 321. The nurse gave me the wrong number. But I didn't realize it until after I entered. So instead of finding my grandfather, there was an elderly woman. It wasn't until I advanced closer that I was able to see her. She'd been covered up with blankets. When I realized my mistake and started walking back toward the door, that's when she called out to me. She called me Robert and told me she had been waiting for me to show up. She said she had something important to talk to me about. Completely ignoring me when I tried to tell her I wasn't this Robert, she laughed and told me to stop messing around, and that she needed my help.

"Seeing as how she wasn't going to give up, I decided to indulge her and listen to what she wanted to tell me. I mean, if she was looking right at me, talking to me, still thinking I was this Robert, then I knew no amount of reasoning was going to convince her otherwise. So I listened to her. That's when she asked me to watch over you, her granddaughter. She pointed to a picture of you in your cap and gown she kept on the bedside table. When I was able to take a better look, I had to admit I was drawn to you on some weird level. There was something in your eyes which called to me."

I stopped talking for a brief moment, assessing how she was handling all of the information. One hand was still covering her mouth, her other resting over her heart. A single tear escaped her eye, and it took everything in me to sit still and finish my story.

"Your grandmother saw me holding your picture and pleaded with me again to help keep you safe. She told me you'd been through a terrible ordeal and she was worried for you. Of course, at the time, I had no idea what she was talking about. But because of my inexplicable draw toward you, and the pleading in the old woman's voice, I simply had to help her. I had to let her know I would watch over you and keep you safe. And it's exactly what I did, from then on."

Knowing she was having a hard time dealing with everything I'd just told her, I tried to deflect some of her confusion by asking her a simple question. Maybe it would help.

"Who was Robert?"

It worked. Some of the disbelief washed away, distracted by a simple question.

"Robert was her younger brother. He passed away in a tragic fire when he was a young man, probably more than fifty years ago now."

I knew the old woman was confused, but I had no idea to what extent. Not until that very moment.

"How did you know where to find me? How did you even get my name?" she asked, curious to find out all the sordid details.

"I was able to obtain your name from one of the nurses who was working that evening. It really didn't take much since she was flirting with me nonstop. So I decided to use it to my advantage and acquire the information I needed."

"But it doesn't explain how you were able to find me, merely based on my grandmother's name."

"You were listed as her emergency contact and next of kin. Plus, they had your address listed, so it really wasn't all that hard."

The look of realization crept over her face. I felt bad spewing all of it at her so quickly, but she needed to know. *I* needed her to know after all these years. Even though I knew I was doing a good thing by keeping my promise and making sure she was safe, I'd still felt a little guilty, watching someone who didn't know I was keeping tabs on them. I actually felt a weight lifted as I revealed the whole story.

"But why didn't you tell her yes then forget about it once you left her room? Why did you feel the need to follow up and start watching me?"

"I don't have an answer that will satisfy you, Sara, because I don't really know myself. Normally, I would've done just that, walked out of her room and chalked it up to a senile old woman. But I couldn't do it, not after looking into her eyes, witnessing how worried and fearful she was for you. I had to keep my promise to her, and keep it I did...for eight years. Actually, I'm still keeping my promise to your grandmother, and I'll continue to keep it for the rest of my life."

After my last statement, she suddenly rose from the couch and made her way over to where I kept the liquor. She poured herself a small glass and drank it quickly, making a face as I'm sure it burned on the way down.

"But if you lived here in Seattle, how were you able to watch me and take all of those photographs?"

The next part of my story wasn't going to go over well.

"I was starting up a new hotel not far from where you lived, so I was able to visit there often enough. But when I wasn't physically there myself, I hired someone to watch over you."

"What? You had someone *else* following me? Was it all the time? Did they report my every move back to you? Did you have a good laugh at my expense, knowing I was none the wiser?" I'd thought she'd calm down after telling her the brunt of my tale, but I was wrong. Her spine stiffened and she looked as if she was preparing for battle.

"Sara, no. It wasn't like that at all. I was trying to keep you safe, especially after everything you went through." She instantly became uncomfortable, even more than she was previously.

"With my connections, I was able to obtain a copy of the police report. But someone wasn't doing their job thoroughly, because it was more generic than anything." She relaxed a little, which made me bristle with awareness. "It listed your name along with his, and his address, the duration of the kidnapping and that you were admitted to the hospital with minimal scrapes and bruises. Then it went on to give the length of his sentence to the institution."

She calmed down even more. "That's it? That's all it said?"

"Yeah. Pretty much. Should it have listed more, Sara?" I knew I shouldn't push, but I couldn't help myself.

"No."

Already knowing she wasn't going to give me more, she switched it up, throwing me off-guard.

"So, what changed?" she asked, placing her empty glass on the table.

"What do you mean?"

"I mean, you were in the background for all those years, so why did you decide now to meet me? Was I a game to you? Did you pity me or something? Get close to the poor, unsuspecting girl. Did it become too much trying to *keep me safe* from a distance that you decided it would be easier to try and control my every action up-close and personal? Because it's exactly what you've been trying to do ever since the first day I met you."

"It was nothing like that, Sara, and I think you know it." Frustration took over. I stood and started pacing back and forth. I hated the thought she didn't trust me, thinking I'd only met her to fulfill some sort of sick fantasy or game or whatever the hell was running through her mind.

"Do I, Alek? Do I know?"

"Yes. All I ever wanted to do was keep you safe. I was drawn to you, for reasons I can't explain. Once I found out you had up and moved—and to *my* city, no less—I took it as a sign I should get to know you. So, I came into the shop and the rest is history."

"But I'd been here for almost a year. Why didn't you meet me sooner?" Based on our entire conversation, her question was odd. But I wouldn't hold it against her because I'd asked myself that same question.

"I fought with myself, thinking it wasn't a good idea to meet you in person. I wanted to keep my distance, thinking it was the safest thing for both of us. But the more time went by and the more I saw you walking down the street, or casually dining in a restaurant, the more my resolve weakened. Until one day... I convinced myself you would be safer with me by your side. Then the more time I spent with you, the more I just had to be with you. Looking back, I'd initially thought it was a mistake I walked into your grandmother's room, but now I realize it was fate."

~6~

Sara

I had no idea what I was going to do with all of the information he gave me. I was beyond livid with him, but was it because he kept the secret from me? Or was it because he'd been watching me all those years? I wasn't quite sure. Maybe it was a mixture of both.

To say I was stunned was an understatement. Of all the scenarios which ran through my mind, that was not one of them. Him walking into my grandmother's room? By accident? It was all too much to comprehend.

But it was his story. Did I believe him?

Without a doubt.

My privacy had been ripped away, and it didn't sit well with me. I was trying to see his side of the situation, but it was still a little cloudy.

As I was starting to come around, having a bit of time to process everything, I was pulled back to the other side of the coin, pissed off he'd hid something of such magnitude from me.

My conflicting emotions were driving me insane.

I had to sort through everything to figure out what I wanted to do next. *Yeah, good luck to me.*

Alek had long since dismissed his driver for the evening. It was his car he drove to drop me off at home, the tension building with each mile.

I wanted to get something off my chest, and it looked like then was as good a time as any. "Alek, I'm still furious with you over the whole stalking thing."

"I wasn't stalking you, Sara, and I think you know it. I was only trying to make sure you were safe at all times."

"All right, I understand it wasn't stalking, per se, but still. How would you feel if you learned someone had been following you for eight years and you knew nothing about it?" I asked, curious to hear what his response would be.

He cocked his head to the side and looked as if he was giving my question some serious thought. Then he said something I didn't expect.

"I would feel sort of violated."

I blanched, and not subtly. "Then why the hell are you making me feel as if my reaction is over-the-top? That I'm blowing this out of proportion?"

"I never once said you didn't have a right to be upset. What I tried to remind you over and over was that everything I did was in your best interest, to keep you out of harm's way. I know I sound like a broken record, Sara. But what's done is done and I can't change any of it, not that I would want to." He mumbled something and gripped the wheel tight, expelling a long sigh.

"What did you say?" I could do nothing but stare at his perfect profile. How I was able to remain upset with the man, yet long for him to hold and kiss me all at the same time, baffled me.

"I said, this is the way it should have always been. I should have been at your side the entire time and not in the shadows." He looked like a man riddled with regret, and I couldn't help but feel for him. *Damn all these emotions.*

Soon, we were pulling up to the front of my apartment.

I wasn't sure if he'd drop me off and leave or if he'd try to walk me up, like I knew he liked to do.

Shutting off his engine, he opened his car door, making his way around to help me from my seat. *I have my answer.* I chose to remain silent, a feat easier said than done. While I'd been crushed to find out Alek had some sort of crazy, possibly dangerous secret, I was never able to escape the way he made me feel. I'd thought about him all the damn time, so much it almost drove me insane. I wanted nothing more than to shut off all emotions toward him. But I couldn't.

Now, it's going to be even harder to escape the web he's drawn me into.

The web of Alek.

How delicious yet precarious.

Walking me to my door, I turned to block his entry inside. He looked hurt, but I didn't care. He'd get over it. Silence loomed between us, neither one really knowing what to say. We'd both had the chance to speak our minds, and everything was laid out there to be devoured and contemplated.

What either one of us was going to do, I'd had no idea.

"I know tonight was a lot for you, Sara. So, in light of everything, I'll give you a week to try and process it all." He leaned closer. "One week."

Before I could respond, he placed his hands on either side of my face, drew me in to him and kissed me.

It was quick.

It was sweet.

It was filled with promises and hope.

~7~

Alek

I'd been true to my word. Seven long days and nights passed, and not once did I pick up the phone to call Sara. She needed the time I promised her, and I knew it. Although it killed me not to at least hear her voice, I knew she would never come back to me if I pushed too soon after revealing my secret.

But that day was the day I'd promised to go and get my woman. Well, I'd promised myself, never telling her anything beyond the fact I was willing to give her a week to sort everything out.

Making sure to finish up any outstanding business I had by two in the afternoon, I grabbed for my cell and dialed her number.

"Hello," she answered, her voice music to my ears. I knew if she hadn't wanted to speak to me, she would have never answered her phone, my name surely popping up on her screen to alert her.

"Hi, Sara. How are you?"

"Fine. How are you?" *Okay, enough chit-chat.*

"Fine, as well. Listen, I wanted to know if I could take you out for a late lunch. Are you hungry?"

"Today?" she asked, a small amount of trepidation in her voice. *Nothing like surprising the hell out of her. Way to go, Devera.*

"Yeah. I'm all finished up at work, and I'm starving." There was silence for a brief moment. "Please don't make me eat alone. People will talk." My voice was light, a chuckle escaping to show her I was trying my best to be casual and airy. *Fuck, this is hard.* All I wanted to do was swing by and steal her for the afternoon. Not ask permission. Just whisk her away before she could refuse. I might have gotten away with it before, but our situation was different. I had to follow the rules, whatever the hell those were, and tread carefully.

One wrong move and she'd run away for good.

"Please," I pleaded again. I needed to get her alone, have her close to me. Knowing I still had a profound effect on her, I needed to remind her of our chemistry. If I had nothing but the physical to go on right then, I'd take it and exploit the shit out of it.

"Okay, yes. Let me talk to Matt quickly and make sure he can close up for me." My jaw twitched hearing his name. "Let me call you right back."

"Sounds good. Talk soon," I said as I ended the call. Pacing my office was a new occurrence for me. People waited on me, not the other way around. But if the person I was waiting for was Sara, then I would suck it up and give her the time she needed.

During our brief time together, I knew she realized I was a bit of a control freak. I liked things done a certain way, and when I asked someone to do something, I'd like them to comply and not give me an argument. Normally, people didn't ignore or refuse me, but Sara was completely different. In no way, shape or form did I want to dictate her every move or control her life. But I *did* want her to listen to me when I asked her to do something if I believed she was entering a situation which wasn't safe or wise.

But all in due time. I couldn't completely change the man I was, but I would try my hardest to rein in my demands a bit, do my best to be reasonable. *Damnit, I hate that word. 'Reasonable.'*

Sara called me back not ten minutes later. Twenty minutes after that, we were headed toward our destination.

~ ~ ~ ~

"Do you own this place, Alek?" she asked as I ushered her through the front door, steering her toward a booth near the back of the restaurant. I brought her there because I knew she'd love the old-world architectural charm. Plus, the lighting was dim, giving way to the perfect setting for something quaint and intimate.

"Actually, yes. Do you like it?" I waited for her to answer as I pulled out her chair. Only once she was nice and cozy did I take my own seat. While sitting directly across from her gave me the best view, I longed to be closer. Clasping my hands together, I rested them on the table and smiled, waiting for her to say something. Anything.

The pure lilt to her voice did strange things to me. It was light and feminine but also strong yet extremely sexy.

"I do. It's really quite beautiful." I couldn't help but become lost in her, probably staring a bit too intently across the table. "What? Why are you looking at me like that?" she asked, nervously shifting in her seat.

Is it wrong I love the fact I can make her uneasy? If she didn't care anything about me at all, she would be truly nonchalant, letting me know exactly what her feelings were for me. But no, she was nervous and it was a good sign.

"Are you sure you want the answer?" I licked my lips in habit but when her eyes flew to my mouth, fixating on it, I smiled and licked them again. The second time on purpose. I would use anything in my arsenal to remind her she wanted to constantly be near me.

"No, I don't. Because whatever you're thinking won't be happening anytime soon, especially not out in the open like this. Even if you *are* the owner." She cocked her brow, a smirk playing nicely on her lovely lips.

Sass. I love it.

"Do I hear a challenge, Ms. Hawthorne?" I couldn't help myself.

She looked stunned for a brief moment but it was washed away when I winked, calming her immediately. I would love nothing than to ravage her, other patrons be damned, but I knew enough not to push too much too quickly.

She did her best to remain stoic. "I think we should focus on lunch." She hid behind her menu, but I saw it. The smile which overtook her beautiful face was too big for me not to notice.

I wondered what she was thinking. Was she picturing herself beneath me? Was she remembering what I tasted like when I ravaged her mouth? Was she remembering what my cock felt like buried deep inside her?

"Alek," she called out, tearing me from my wayward thoughts.

"Oh, sorry. Did you ask me something?"

Her face looked so cute all scrunched up. "Yes, I did. Where were you just now? What were you thinking about?"

I'm picturing fucking you.

"You." I'd told the truth, leaving out a few minor details.

"Well, I'm right here," she said, reaching across the table and brushing her fingers over the top of my hand. But she pulled away quickly, not lingering for too long.

"What did you ask me?"

The waitress interrupted us before she could answer, standing a little too close to me to be appropriate. I ignored her, all of my focus on the gorgeous woman across from me.

"Can I bring you something to drink, Mr. Devera?" she asked as she leaned in to me, completely ignoring Sara.

Still never making eye contact with the brazen woman, I looked at Sara and said, "What would you like to drink, sweetheart?"

Sara blinked quickly before simply replying, "Unsweetened tea, please."

Finally glancing up at the waitress, I said, "I'll have what she's having." I smiled at the awe-struck woman, letting her know I was clearly taken by someone, and that someone definitely not being her.

Once we were alone again, I repeated my question. "What did you ask me before?"

I touched her leg under the table with my foot, pretending as if I was simply getting comfortable. But I saw what I'd done to her. She stumbled over her words, trying her best to right herself.

"I...uh...I asked you about your family."

"What would you like to know?"

"You mentioned before you had a sister. Can you tell me a little more about her?" Her question was innocent enough, but it made me uncomfortable just the same. I never talked about my sister. It was too painful, her memory torturing yet comforting me from time to time.

I didn't want to be rude, but I certainly wasn't in the mood to discuss something as heavy as my late sister. "Maybe another time." I couldn't help but notice her look of disappointment. I knew she was trying to get to know me better, which was great, but there were some topics which were off-limits for the time being. "What else would you like to know? Ask away."

Showing her I was open to talking about other things, she instantly relaxed and dove right in. "What about your parents? Are they still living?"

"No, they both passed on quite a few years ago. My father died when I was younger, much like your mother did. Unfortunately we have that in common. Losing a parent is never easy, especially when you're young. They miss out on so many milestones, don't they?"

She simply nodded.

"Anyway, my mother passed about twelve years ago. She'd gone in for a routine surgery and contracted an infection. It spread throughout her body, killing her three days later."

"Oh, my God, Alek. I'm so sorry."

I couldn't hide the sad look in my eyes, allowing Sara to witness a small part of my sorrow, something I'd kept hidden from everyone else. "Thanks," I simply said. "I think she gave up the will to live after my sister..." I trailed off, not even wanting to say the word *died*. Once I took a much needed deep breath, I continued. "Thankfully, I was close to my grandfather, spending all my time with him and learning everything I could. He'd inherited his money from his father before him. But instead of doing what I did and opening up businesses, he gave a lot of it away to charities he was passionate about. He loved helping others, a trait I truly admired about him."

Sara reached across the table again and grabbed my hand. "He sounded like a great man."

"He was."

Before we could continue our conversation, the waitress approached with our drinks. Placing them on the table in front of us, I saw her eyes land on our clasped hands, a look of displeasure written all over her face.

This woman needs a course in subtlety.

"Do you want to hear the specials today, Mr. Devera?" she asked as she pushed her tits out further into my personal space. I glanced over at Sara and saw the look on her face. She clearly didn't like the woman.

This is good. Very good indeed. It means she cares.

"That won't be necessary," I answered. "Sara, what would you like to eat?"

"What's good here? Do you have any recommendations?" Her gaze relaxed off our waitress and flew to her menu, intently searching for something to choose.

"The salmon is amazing, but they also make a mean filet mignon, if that's what you are hungry for instead. But if you're not sure, I can order for us both, if you like," I offered.

She agreed with a nod.

After the waitress left, Sara surprised me with what came out of her mouth. I knew she didn't particularly care for the woman, but I never expected her to say anything to me about it.

"I'm surprised our waitress actually left," she said, her tone indicating obvious jealousy.

Again, this is very good.

"Why do you say that?" I asked, playing dumb. I wanted to hear what she'd say next.

"Don't act like you didn't notice her blatantly flirting with you, right in front of me."

"Nope, didn't notice her at all, actually. I only have eyes for you Sara. How many times do I have to tell you this?"

Oh, I'm good.

I reached for her other hand and thankfully she gave it to me. I ran my thumbs across her knuckles, reveling in the feel of her soft skin. The longer we touched, the hotter my desire simmered just below the surface.

Our waitress returned relatively quickly, our food in tow. She glanced at me caressing Sara's hands, shooting her an annoyed look before turning her eyes to me.

I didn't even acknowledge her.

Keeping hold of Sara's hands, I simply raised them up as the waitress served us.

Once she was gone, I reluctantly broke our connection.

"Shall we?" I asked, grabbing my cutlery and preparing to dig in.

"This looks really good."

"Wait until you try it then." I smiled and placed my first forkful into my mouth. "What are you waiting for? Dig in."

I didn't think she even realized she was staring at me, my words jolting her out of whatever thoughts were running through her head. She placed a small piece of salmon on her tongue, a small moan escaping in the process.

"You like?" *If she keeps making those noises each time she takes a bite, I'm going to be forced to bend her over the table and take what's mine.*

Not being able to form a complete sentence, she simply mumbled, "Uh-huh."

I laughed and continued eating. I understood completely. They had the best salmon around.

After the majority of our meal was consumed, I didn't waste any time asking her the question I'd been dying to pose for the past hour. "Do you have any plans for next Friday?"

"No," she answered right away, gasping as if she hadn't meant to answer so quickly. Especially since she had no idea why I'd asked.

"I have to attend a charity dinner and wanted to know if you would be my date." I hoped I hadn't come across nervous, the fear of her refusing always a reality.

She hesitated a moment before answering, her eyes searching my face for something. What, I had no idea, but she could look all she wanted if it meant she would agree to accompany me. "I'd love to. What's it for?" she asked as she took the last bite of her delicious meal. I think she'd agree to just about anything, her love of her food tipping things in my favor.

"It's a charity for domestic violence."

Her brows almost hit her hairline, her look telling me how much my statement shocked the hell out of her.

"What? You didn't expect me to be involved in something which actually had merit? Maybe a charity for struggling yacht club members would be more my speed?"

The look on her face was priceless. "No...it's not that. I...uh..."

I put her out of her misery.

"It's all right. I'm only having a bit of fun with you. It's fine, really."

Nervously looking down at her lap, she fussed for a minute before meeting my eyes again. "I don't currently own anything which would be appropriate. I'll have to buy something, but I would have a better idea if I knew exactly what type of dress was required."

"It's a black tie event, so you'll need a gown of sorts. But don't worry about any of the details because I'll take you to buy it." I knew her well enough to know she was going to give me a hard time, ever the proud woman. "Don't try to tell me no, Sara. I'm asking you to be my date, so it's only fair you allow me to buy you the dress." Her mouth parted as if preparing to argue, so I cut her off before the breath left her beautiful lips. "I won't take no for an answer," I said, hoping I wasn't coming across too curt.

"Fine." Thank God she didn't argue with me. We'd been having such a nice lunch, I'd hate to taint it with her stubbornness, no matter how much her feistiness turned me on.

"That was easy enough. I wish you were so agreeable all the time."

"Yeah, that'll never happen." She smirked.

"A man can dream, can't he?"

Unfortunately, before our light banter could continue, our inappropriate waitress appeared again. "Would you like any dessert tonight?" The question was really only poised at me, since she didn't glance in Sara's direction when she asked. She couldn't care less she was occupying the same table.

Before I could dismiss our rude server, words fell from Sara's lips, causing me to stifle my laughter...and shock.

"Honey, are you trying to offer up *yourself* as dessert to Mr. Devera? Because I can assure you he doesn't want any of it." She leaned closer to the intruder. "None at all. So, if you would simply give us the check, we will be on our way."

I couldn't help it.

I smiled.

Big.

The rude woman's jaw hit the table, but she quickly gathered herself and stalked off in a huff.

"Wow. Where did *that* come from?" I dared to ask. There was no mistaking my pleasure at her outburst. It only drove home how much she cared, her jealousy like a stamp of ownership all over me.

"Sorry. I normally wouldn't say anything, but I couldn't take her brazenness one more second. I simply had to say something. I mean, come on, she was being so freaking obvious, coming on to you every time she came over here."

I continued to smile, shaking my head in amusement.

"What?" she asked, confusion plastered all over her face. She looked so beautiful, trying to hide a cluster of emotions. Our waitress had clearly riled her up, anger dancing on her brow. But confusion was there also, mainly at me. I was sure she wanted to know what I'd found so funny.

"I like the fact you're jealous over me. It makes me feel good. Makes me feel wanted."

There was no time for her to respond because we'd been interrupted once again. Out of the corner of my eye, I'd seen the waitress talking to the manager. He'd come over in a hurry to give me the bill, no doubt trying to quell any forthcoming issue.

Quickly glancing down at the piece of paper, I grabbed a wad of bills from my wallet and threw everything back in the receipt holder.

"If you're the owner, why are you paying for the meal? Can't you write if off or something?"

"If I didn't pay for anything at any of my businesses, well, I wouldn't have any money, I suppose." I smiled again, stood up and held my hand out for her. When her fingers touched my palm, I'd felt a warmth only she could give me. It was wonderful. Magical even, although I didn't think I'd ever used such a word in my entire life.

As we walked toward the front door, I wrapped my arm around her waist and pulled her close, kissing her temple. What I'd really wanted to do was claim her mouth, but I'd thought better of it, not wanting to act too fast too soon.

On the drive home, all I could think about was how to make things right between us again. I was trying my best to do the whole nice-and-slow dance, but it was driving me insane. I hated that I'd fucked up so much her trust in me had been shaken. But I'd do whatever it took to make her fully come back to me, trusting me once more.

I had to go away again for business, hating to leave her alone, now more than ever. She was still fragile and if someone said the wrong thing to her, warning her against giving me another shot, I didn't know what I'd do.

Hell, I don't even know if she told anyone about what happened. Other than Alexa, of course.

"I'll be away until Saturday. But as soon as I come back, we'll make plans to shop for your dress. Sound good?" I asked, glancing to my right, her profile making my heart beat faster.

Her eyes connected with mine. "Yeah."

My second-favorite four letter word.

~8~

Sara

The days flew by in a blur. Full Bloom and Alek had kept me quite busy. True to his promise, he took me to purchase a beautiful gown for his charity event. Thankfully, he tore the dress from my hands and gave it to the clerk before I'd had the opportunity to look at the price tag. He knew me well enough to figure out I was going to argue with him about buying it if I'd seen the cost.

The beautiful garment hung in my closet. Each time I saw it, butterflies danced in my belly. I promised him I would go with him, but as the days crept up, the more nervous I became. I never thought on it too long, always closing the closet door quickly, trapping the gown inside, along with my nerves.

Until the next time I opened it, of course.

My initial anger toward Alek and the secret he kept from me was dissipating, knowing in my heart he was only doing what he thought was right. He'd promised to never lie to me again, and I took him at his word.

We'd been out several times in the past week, dinners mostly. It made sense, since we both had to eat, and it gave us an opportunity to really talk. Discussing everything from work, to books to what our individual plans were for the future, both personal and work-related, ate up the time. I hated when he dropped me off because it meant I was going to be alone.

Again.

But I wasn't going to rush jumping back into bed with him. Thankfully, he must've felt the same way, never pressing beyond a goodnight kiss.

~ ~ ~ ~

The date for the fundraiser was upon me. I would finally be able to wear the beautiful fabric, accompanying the one man who was slowly weaving his way back into my heart.

I'd still had mixed feelings about attending. On one hand, I wanted to stand by his side, the cause something he obviously cared about, but on the other hand, I knew I'd be uncomfortable surrounded by his type of people.

The insanely rich.

He'd told me the charity gala was to be held at his main hotel, located right there in Seattle. After doing a bit of my own research on his charities, I discovered the one that evening would surely bring out the who's who of Seattle's richest players. Needless to say, I was more and more intimidated with each passing second. I didn't fit in to his world; one glance at me and those people would know it. Not wanting to be uncomfortable the entire evening, nor wanting to disappoint or embarrass Alek, I decided to give him a call.

There was still some time before we were set to arrive. Enough time to back out and hopefully for him to find another date, although the mere thought was like poison to me.

I could return the dress, shoes and clutch he purchased.

No harm, no foul.

I called his cell but it just rang then went to voicemail. I left a message telling him I was unable to make it and that I was sorry. I didn't divulge too many details, not wanting to give him ammunition to try and talk me out of it, which he would surely do.

Placing the ringer on silent, I set the phone down on my nightstand. If I answered, he would definitely be able to convince me to change my mind.

Needing to release some of my nervous tension, I decided to take a nice hot shower. While in there, I followed through with my normal routine of washing my hair and shaving. At least I would be nice and clean for my night of relaxation.

I stepped from the bathroom and into the hallway when I ran into a hard body. I didn't even have to look up to know who it was, his scent infiltrating my defenses instantly.

"How did you get in here, Alek?" I said, stunned he was really standing in front of me. When I was able to reel in my shock a little, it was then I was met with an extraordinary sight.

Alek in his glorious, designer tuxedo.

The more I stared at him, the more I slipped into some kind of daze. After some of the longest seconds known to man, I averted my eyes, needing to keep my head straight if I was going to successfully engineer my way out of the night's engagement.

I realized I was in for an argument without him even uttering a single syllable.

"Key."

"What?" I mumbled, completely confused.

"You asked me how I got in. I still have the key you gave me."

"Oh." I completely forgot I'd given him one.

We were still standing in the hallway, toe to toe simply staring at one another. *What's supposed to happen next?* I wasn't sure.

"Excuse me," I mumbled. I needed to throw on some clothes or I feared I was going to jump him, something I wasn't quite ready for yet. Or was I?

Most of my thoughts were consumed with the memories of Alek and me entangled together. Him driving himself deep inside me, making me scream out his name. Every time he kissed me, I longed for nothing more than to take it further, but I'd always stopped myself.

But he was in my personal space in a freaking tux, looking beyond gorgeous, and sex emanating from every fine-ass pore on his body. We stood there, in the hallway, gazing at each other, making no further effort to move from our current positions.

As my lustful thoughts took hold, I realized I was standing in front of him with nothing but a towel wrapped around me. As if he'd sensed my realization, his eyes slowly raked over my entire form, head to toe, a sexy smirk curving the corners of his mouth.

Once he was visually sated, he stepped aside and allowed me the space I needed. Without saying anything further, I maneuvered toward my bedroom so I could at least get dressed. I figured he would give me some privacy while I changed, but I quickly found out I'd figured wrong.

Following directly behind me, he entered my bedroom with me.

"Do you mind if I throw some clothes on?" I pivoted around on my heel and locked him in my gaze once more.

"I've licked and sucked every inch of you. I've been buried so deep in you I thought I would never resurface. Why all of a sudden are you being modest around me?"

Where the hell is this coming from? We'd been taking it slow recently, yet he was acting as if we'd just had sex over and over again.

When I didn't say anything, he simply replied, "I'll wait out in the living room." He was halfway out into the hallway when he turned around quickly, blocking me from shutting my bedroom door all the way. "Oh, and I want to talk about the voicemail you left." Then he sauntered toward the living room.

Crap! I should have known better than to think he would listen to his phone, not give it a second thought, and continue on to the event without me.

I took off my towel and threw on a robe. Leaving my room, I slowly made my way toward Alek. As I approached, he was casually sitting on the couch, his left arm slung over the back of it.

I'd been mentally preparing my argument in my head, but him looking so scrumptious threw me off.

I didn't waste any time, diving right into our inevitable conversation. "Alek, I don't think it's wise for me to accompany you tonight. I've read about these charitable events, and for God's sake, there's a red carpet and paparazzi. It's just not a world I fit into. Not now. Not ever. I would embarrass myself and you in the process. I'm sorry, really I am." I looked away, staring at my feet. "I'll return the dress and everything else as soon as I can."

"Are you finished, Sara?"

"Yes, I suppose I am." Wow, he seemed to be taking what I'd said pretty well. Not as much resistance as I would have thought.

"Now, let me tell you something." *Okay, so I spoke too soon.* "You *do* belong there because you belong with me. You have absolutely nothing to be embarrassed about. Most of the people who are going are uptight and boring. I *need* you there with me, to help me through it."

"But I'm not used to rubbing elbows with those types of people, Alek."

"Do you feel uncomfortable around me? Because I run in the same circles as many of those people." He rose from the couch and walked toward me.

"I don't feel uncomfortable with you because I know you. Plus, I doubt there is anyone else like you." A smile found its way to my lips, even though I fought to remain as serious as possible.

"That is true, but still...you'll be fine. Just trust me." He pulled me into his warm embrace without another word. Whenever I was in his arms, I couldn't think straight. I would agree to almost anything.

It *would* be nice to get all dressed up and spend more time with him. But I still wasn't convinced, not all the way. Before I could let my uneasiness completely take over, he leaned down and kissed me. Since he was allowing me to take the lead with our fresh-start relationship, his lips simply rested on top of mine. I turned it into something more, snaking my hands around the back of his neck and pulling him closer. An all-too-consuming passion took hold, and I let loose.

Moaning into his mouth made him tense up before relaxing and unleashing his own desire.

"Alek," I groaned, breaking our kiss for a moment. "How about we stay here tonight," I teased, leaning back in and capturing his mouth.

"We could really enjoy one another." Lightly nipping his bottom lip, I gripped his arms and tried my best to entice him.

I would allow him to ravage me because I was tired of waiting. But I also wanted to finagle my way out of going to the charity event.

I think he was on to my devious plan, though, because he backed away, spun me around and smacked my ass.

Hard.

"Ow!" I yelled. "What the hell was that for?" Backing up, my feet shuffled across the floor as my hand rubbed my poor, affected cheek.

"That was for trying to trick me, sweetheart. Now, go get dressed before we're late."

The last thing I saw was a huge smile on his face as I disappeared around the corner.

~9~

Sara

It took me longer to slip into my floor-length emerald green gown than it did to do my hair and makeup. Wearing an updo with only a few cascading tendrils made the bare neckline pop, elongating my neck and making me look sexy.

The back of my outfit dipped lower than what I was used to, dangerously on the verge of being indecent, but not quite. The material hugged my body like a second skin, all while remaining classy. The bodice was fitted, pushing my breasts up into a view which simply worked with the ensemble.

Once I slipped on my heels and grabbed my clutch, I made my way out to the living room where Alek was patiently waiting for me.

As soon as I entered the room, his eyes instantly found mine. The air between us was stifled, sexual tension and desire floating all around us.

His breath faltered.

It made me smile.

I knew I looked good, but the way he admired me made me feel like the sexiest woman in the world.

Apparently he likes my dress.

"Sara, you look...breathtaking. You're actually making me rethink taking you out in public tonight." He advanced a few paces. "I don't want any other man to bask in your complete and utter beauty. But alas, we must attend, so it seems I'll have to restrain myself and do my best to make it through the evening." *I swear he'll have a smile plastered on his face the whole night.*

"Oh. One more thing." He reached for a small box sitting on top of the kitchen island. As I stepped closer, I noticed the wording *Cartier*.

Opening it, he extended it so I could take a look. A close look. What I saw made my eyes bulge. It was beautiful, but I prayed he hadn't bought such an extravagant gift for me.

It was simply too much.

Emeralds and diamonds danced together, linked in one huge circle.

"Do you like it?" he asked.

Before I could respond, he took it and brought it around my neck, clasping it and running his fingers over my shoulders as he walked around to stand in front of me.

"Don't worry. I can see that look in your eye. It's merely a loan. Although, if you want, I can definitely buy it for you. Just say the word."

"It's on loan?" I asked as I ran my hand gently over the precious stones. "Like in *Pretty Woman?*"

"*Pretty Woman?*" he asked. "I assume it's a movie."

"You've never seen it? Oh, you don't know what you're missing." Without letting him speak another word, I launched into my tirade over one of my favorite movies. "It's about this prostitute who meets this rich guy, and he hires her for the week, and she changes him then they fall in love, and he rescues her on her balcony even though he's afraid of heights." I took a much needed breath. "It's very romantic."

The look on his face was priceless. "Sounds...um...interesting. I'm assuming somewhere in the movie he gives her a necklace?"

"Oh, yes. When he takes her to the opera." He smiled, amused by the faraway look on my face. "Why are you looking at me like that?"

"You're rather stunning when you're excited about something, rambling on about this movie being no exception."

Another minute passed before he extended his arm and asked, "Shall we?"

~~~~

We arrived directly in the midst of the fluttering cameras. Alek had already warned me, rubbing my back to try to calm the rising nerves.

"Just breathe, baby. You'll do great."

Holding on to him, we headed toward the front of the hotel. I tried
my best to smile as we made our way through the throng of people,
stopping every now and then to catch my breath. Between the dress
and the flashing lights, I was caught off-balance more times than I'd
wanted to count. But all in all, everything went smoothly.

Until I heard some rude man yell out, "Who's the flavor of the week,
Mr. Devera?"

I'm sure it was done to garner a reaction, not only from him but me,
as well. They'd almost succeeded. Alek instantly tensed, and as he
started toward the ballsy photographer, I gripped his hand and pulled
him in to me.

"Alek, don't give him the satisfaction. It's exactly what he wants.
Please...please, don't give it to him." I was holding on for dear life
because I wasn't sure what he would end up doing. Eventually, he
turned toward me and as soon as his eyes found mine, he physically
relaxed.

We made a beeline for the door. Many paces later and we were
ensconced in the ballroom where the event was being held. Rich
tones of red, browns and golds made for an over-the-top elegant room.
People milled all around the expansive area, conversing and
networking with one another.

Alek was intently surveying everyone in sight. No sooner did he
make eye contact with someone before they filtered toward him,

shaking his hand and praising him on how the event turned out. He made sure to introduce me to everyone who approached. Most of them were polite enough, telling me it was nice to meet me before quickly moving on to gush over the man attached to my side. There were some who simply nodded in my direction without even uttering a word.

I could feel the men giving me a once-over, as did their women, the looks being quite different. The men were not subtle as they perused my body while the women looked me up and down, a look of annoyance in their uptight glances. Alek must've caught on, because he ended most of the conversations rather quickly.

A little while later a distinguished couple approached us. I noticed something different about them almost instantly.

They seemed...nice.

"Alek, how are you, son?" the man greeted as he took hold of Alek's hand, pulling him in for a tight hug. There was a familiarity which passed between them, appearing genuinely happy to see one another.

"Mr. Collins. How nice to see you." Alek turned his attention to the gentleman's wife, leaning forward to kiss her cheek. "Mrs. Collins. How are you both?" There was a longing in his eyes. Almost as if he was living in the past, if only for a brief moment.

"We are very well. And how many times do we have to insist you call us by our first names and stop with all of this formalness?"

"Old habits die hard." He laughed.

Both of them glanced back and forth between myself and the man crowding my personal space, waiting for him to introduce me.

As if on cue, Alek regained his manners and spoke up. "Sorry, I apologize. Please let me introduce you to a very special woman. This is my girlfriend, Sara. Sara, this is Brad and Natalie Collins."

To say I was surprised would be an understatement. We hadn't discussed the true nature of our relationship in the days which followed my discovery of his secret.

Yes, I'd agreed to be his girlfriend. But that was before the shit hit the fan.

I wasn't going to correct him, however. Especially not in front of anyone. It was kind of nice to know he still desired to put a label on me. On us.

Knowing myself, I was sure I would bring it up later on, trying my best to figure out where we stood, once and for all. If I'd forgiven him then we needed to move forward.

Question was, had I?

Brad reached out to me first, then his wife, both pulling me into a big hug. It took me by surprise how forward they were, but I didn't mind. Not at all. There was something so warm and inviting about the two of them. They seemed down-to-earth and genuine. It was quite refreshing.

"It's nice to meet both of you," I said. Since setting foot inside the hotel earlier, they were the first people I actually wanted to have a conversation with.

While Brad chatted with Alek, his wife leaned in closer to me, vying for my attention.

"So, sweetheart, how long have you and Alek been together?"

"Not long." I couldn't think of what else to add to my answer. Even though I instantly liked them, I wasn't sure how much information I should reveal.

"Well, you must be pretty special. Alek has never introduced us to a girlfriend of his before, not that he's had many. And we've known him since he was a young boy. He only dates, forever the bachelor. I was wondering when he was going to get serious and start to settle down." Her smile was telling, as if she was privy to a delicious secret. "Alek will forever hold a special place in our hearts," she continued, her smile never vanishing. "He's so incredibly thoughtful."

"How do you mean?" I asked, trying my best to keep her talking.

"I had surgery a little while back, and the same day I was brought home, there was a huge array of calla lilies waiting for me when I arrived. He remembered they're my favorite flowers. He's so quick to think of others, doing his best to make them happy."

Holy shit! She *was the one he came into the shop that first time to buy flowers for?* I shook my head slightly, lost in my own memory of a time which seemed so long ago. I was about to blurt out something but luckily held back, not wanting to burst the poor woman's bubble. It was actually Katherine who created her arrangement of lilies. Alek had nothing to do with it. Well...he paid for it. And had it delivered.

Okay, so he had a big part in it.

Natalie cleared her throat, trying her best to gain my attention again. I had lost myself in the past and it was rude. Garnering all of my focus back on to her, I spoke up. "Well, I really like him, and we're having a great time getting to know each other." Feeling as if it was a prime opportunity to gain some more knowledge about him, I casually pressed her for more information. "How do you know Alek again?"

"We were close friends with his parents. We all practically grew up together." She looked off in the distance for a split-second, as if she was remembering a time long ago. But she caught herself quickly enough and returned her stare to me. "It was such a tragedy what happened to their daughter, to Alek's sister. Just tragic." Breaking eye contact again for a spot in time, she said, "But this is no time to dwell on heartache. This is a time to celebrate all of the good work he's doing with his charity."

We chatted for a little while longer about the upcoming evening when nature knocked on my door. When I found a small lull in our conversation, I jumped all over it. "If you'll excuse me, I have to find a restroom.

"Sure thing, honey." Before I turned around, she added, "Hopefully, Alek will bring you by our house for dinner sometime."

"I would like that." Placing my hand on her upper arm, I finished with, "It was a pleasure to meet you."

As I moved closer to the men, I heard Brad say, "Your sister would be so proud of what you are doing here." While Alek tried to put on a brave face, I knew talking about his deceased sibling was difficult for him, even to people he'd known forever. His smile started to falter the longer they stood together.

When neither one of them spoke again, I swooped right in. Rising on my tippy toes, I leaned in close to his ear, my warm breath fanning over him as I asked, "Alek, I have to use the ladies room. Do you know where one is?"

I wasn't dumb. I knew what I was doing to him. My little gesture caused his posture to straighten even more, his chest expanding with the deep breath he inhaled. And while I wanted nothing more than to stand there and engage in a silent battle of sexual games, I desperately needed some time to myself. I needed to regroup and garner enough emotional energy to succumb to the rest of the evening. Never mind the fact my bladder was complaining and would surely revolt if I didn't find the restroom soon.

His hand rested on my lower back as he ushered me across the ballroom floor. Lightly running his thumb back and forth over the small area of naked skin, he teased me more than he knew.

Sensing his touch was slowly undoing me, he tried to reassure me. Certainly he knew how uncomfortable I was, even though I tried my best to blend in. Put on the face he needed. Show my undying support for the man who twisted up every emotion inside me.

As we approached the restrooms, he halted his steps and grabbed hold of my elbow. "Are you okay?" he asked, surely already knowing the answer. "I know most of these people can be a bit much, but you're handling yourself like a champ."

Because I didn't wish to ruin an evening which was apparently important to him, I continued on with my farce. Plastering the best smile imaginable on my face, I raised my head and answered him. "I'm fine. Really. I'm all right. Don't worry about me." I relaxed a little, realizing I had told him the truth. With him by my side, he put all of my crazy fears and nervous anticipations to rest. I found I had the strength to do just about anything.

It was a strange feeling, one I'd been missing since before I left him.

No, before I *ran* from him.

My fake smile was replaced with a genuine one.

Leaning down, he gave me the sweetest kiss. The most reassuring gesture of faith. Faith I would be just fine. Not only that night but going forward with each day which lay ahead of me.

Of us.

"Do you want me to grab you a drink? For when you come back?"

"Sure. How about a glass of wine?" I was sure a nice glass of fermented grapes would help me cope with the barrage of stares which were going to continue to come my way.

"Absolutely. I'll be waiting right here for you, so take your time."

I exited the stall when I'd finished taking care of business and was in the middle of freshening my face when the door opened and closed behind me. Not giving it a second thought, I continued with reapplying my lip gloss.

I was mid-stroke when my body bristled with awareness. The area was certainly large enough, so I knew I wasn't in anyone's way, taking up too much space or any such silly notion. I glanced up into the mirror directly in front of me. My eyes connected with a blonde-haired woman, standing off to my left, glaring at me.

She was rather beautiful, her long hair cascading all around her, soft curls showcasing her glorious mane. Decked out in a long, tight, black gown, she surely caught the attention of most men.

Where my gown was sexy yet tasteful, hers defied all appropriateness. The dip in her gown showed too much of her breasts, threatening a nip slip if she moved the wrong way. But while her attire was questionable, I also knew she was wealthy.

Which was probably why she'd been able to pull off such a dress.

Money.

It forgave even the mistakes of fashion.

Her face looked familiar, but for some reason, I couldn't place where I'd known her from.

The fact I couldn't recall was upsetting. I didn't want to appear rude, but then again that award would go to Miss Ignorant, who was boring holes of contempt straight through me.

What the hell is her problem? Are we wearing the same gown? No. Did I accidentally bump into her out on the floor? No.

How could I have known what the issue was when I simply didn't know her?

"Can I help you with something?" I asked, acid weaving in my tone. The more she glowered at me, the more confident I was giving it right back to her.

"You're here with Alek, right?"

Lightbulb went off.

That voice.

She was the woman who'd been hanging all over Alek at the bar the one time I'd run into him while out with Matt and Alexa.

What the hell is her name again? Lucinda?

"Yes, I am. But apparently from the obvious way you keep sneering at me, you don't like that fact. Am I right?" I really didn't need her to respond, the answer clearly written all over her scornful face.

"Considering you're only the flavor of the week, I really couldn't care less," she said as she faked a bored look, inspecting her nails as if the mere thought of talking to me was of no significance at all. "He'll tire of you soon enough. Then he'll come back to me."

Why did she have to use the same terminology the ignorant reporter used earlier? *Flavor of the week.* I didn't want her words to hurt, but they stung like a bitch.

Before my brain could come up with a retort, she turned on her heel, whipped open the door and strode out as if I was nothing. No more than a nuisance who had to be dealt with. The lowest of the low, according to *her* snooty ass, at least.

Trying my best to reel it in before I went back out there, I took a deep breath and mumbled to myself. "You can do this, Sara. You can get through this evening. Ignore that bitch. Alek's with you." I looked at myself in the mirror, my uncertain amber eyes staring back at me. I heard the words. I wanted to believe them, but she had succeeded in making me doubt myself.

Did Alek always go back to her? He'd told me they'd only slept together once. Did he lie to me? Was she lying?

I wouldn't know anything until I left the bathroom.

I blew out one more breath before my fingers circled around the door handle. Pulling it open, I held my head high and strode out toward the ballroom.

Toward the man who was certainly going to be answering some questions.

~10~

Sara

Alek was standing near the end of the bar, his eyes glued in my direction as if he'd been waiting for me to emerge.

Once he saw me walking toward him, he pushed off the bar and met me in the middle. "Are you okay, Sara? I was on my way to get your drink and I saw Jacinda come out of there." I couldn't hide the hurt look on my face, no matter how much I tried or how strong I wished to appear. "Did she say something to you?"

I didn't know how else to tell him but to just blurt it all out. "She called me your flavor of the week and said when you tire of me, you'll make your way back to her." Even speaking the words stung. Mainly because I had no idea whether or not she was lying. It seemed I was about to find out. "She's the woman from the bar, the one who was hanging all over you that night, right?" I didn't need him to answer. I remembered her name falling from his lips when he was trying to convince me they weren't together.

"Don't listen to a damn thing she says, Sara. She's upset she can't entice me into her clutches again. Once was enough, trust me." And there it was. Him reminding me of their sexual tryst.

My silence was enough for him to pull me close, trying his best to soothe me with his strength and affection. "I mean it. Don't pay attention to her. She's just bitter."

"Bitter she can't have you? Again?" I hated he slept with her, but I hated it even more that images of them together were creeping into my thoughts.

I really need a glass of wine. Now.

"Yes. I've refused all of her advances, and it drives her insane she can't turn my affections to her. I only have eyes for you. Please, trust me when I tell you that. You have nothing to worry about."

His arm wrapped around my waist, the fabric from my gown brushing against his tux. Being close to him always reassured me. Not wanting to discuss *her* any further, I changed the subject.

"I'd like that wine now, please." Without further hesitation, he led me across the floor to the table we were sitting at. Once I was seated, he made his way to the bar to grab my much needed glass of escape. The people who were sitting with us were engaged in their own conversations, glancing over at me every now and then. I tried not to make eye contact with them. If they had no interest in conversing with me, then I had no time for them either.

Glancing around the room, I took in the sights of the various people, all gathered for one common reason. The dress attire was something I only saw in magazines. I'd never been surrounded by so many beautiful and wealthy people before in my entire life.

I was busy watching a younger couple interacting not fifty feet from where I was seated. She looked as if she was angry with him for some reason, her attitude written all over her face, although she made sure to keep her voice low enough so no one would hear. I couldn't fathom why she would be upset. She was all dressed up, a handsome man on her arm and not a care in the world. Or so I thought. Until I saw another woman walk by, her handsome date's attention following the passerby with every step she took. *He has a wandering eye. Oh, the nerve.* I didn't know what I would do if Alek behaved in such a way in front of me. *Actually, yes I do. I wouldn't put up with it, plain and simple.*

Lost in the make-believe scenario in my head, a voice startled me enough to make me jump.

A stranger's voice.

"You're quite the talk of the night, my dear." A man with a raspy voice leaned close to my ear, hinting at a familiarity which didn't really exist between the two of us. When I turned my head to find out who had been so brazen to invade my personal space, I was stunned to find the culprit was a good-looking man. He appeared to be in his mid- to late-thirties, tall with a slimmer yet toned build. His dark hair and bright blue eyes melted many a heart, I was sure. There was no doubt the man turned his share of heads.

But there was something familiar about him I couldn't quite put my finger on.

"And why might that be, may I ask?" He seemed nice enough, so I thought it only polite to engage him. Plus, he was the first one who had actually sought out a conversation with me, so I took advantage.

"Isn't it obvious? You're hands-down the most beautiful woman here. Every man is looking at you with lustful want, and every woman is jealous." He leaned back and extended his hand to me. I turned around fully in my chair to accept his gesture. "I'm Cameron. Cameron Devera."

"Devera?"

"Yes. Alek is my cousin. Our fathers were brothers." It was then it made perfect sense why he'd had a familiar air about him. There was definitely a family resemblance, although he wasn't quite in the same league as Alek. Then again, I didn't think any man alive was in the same league as Alek.

"Nice to meet you, Cameron. I'm Sara." Still holding my palm in his, he raised it to his lips and placed a gentle kiss upon my soft skin. As he was releasing my hand, Alek appeared behind him, placing a firm grip on the man's neck. But Cameron didn't flinch, probably because he expected his cousin's reaction.

"Don't even think about it, Cameron. She's with me, so keep your hands, and eyes, off her." His smile was deceptive, appearing as if he was happy to see his relative, but the venom in his voice told a different story. There was simply no mistaking his warning.

"Wouldn't even think about it, cousin. Just being friendly." Cameron focused on me again before he made his retreat. "It was a pleasure to meet you, Sara. Until next time." The comment garnered a snarl from Alek. Again, not really a shocker. Although, I would've thought he'd act differently around his family.

"Nice to meet you, as well, Cameron," I said as he walked away.

Alek kept his eye on the man until he was sure he was no longer within hearing range. When he turned to look back at me, he seemed annoyed.

"What is the matter with you?" I asked. "Why were you so rude to him?"

"Just because we're blood doesn't mean anything, Sara. I don't trust him as far as I can throw him. Please, do me a favor and steer clear of him for the rest of the night." The more he spoke, the more angry he was becoming, and I had no idea why. "He'll go out of his way to get to you, especially now he knows you're with me."

"Don't you think you're making too much of this? All he was doing was making small talk." I knew instantly he was going to answer me, a twinge of anger sure to weave its way into his reply.

"No, I'm not overreacting at all. He wasn't simply 'making small talk' with you. He was feeling you out, to see how far he could push you. Thank God I came over when I did."

Okay. I had no idea what his issue was with Cameron, but I sure as hell wasn't going to be caught in the middle of it. I didn't see anything wrong with having a conversation with someone, especially since everyone else had ignored me so far. He was making me feel guilty for no reason at all.

"Oh, yeah, Alek. Thank the heavens above you arrived when you did. If he was here any longer, he might have been able to convince me to take my clothes off, right here in front of everyone." I was not going to curtail my annoyance with him. Not at all.

"You're not funny. Not one bit," he snapped. His reaction continued to surprise me, even though I knew I was pushing him toward it. His fists were clenched at his sides and he was trying his best to calm down. Doing a good job of appearing unaffected, I knew he was anything but. His face may not have shown any signs of distress, but if anyone paid any attention at all to his body language, they could clearly see he was pissed off.

Since I didn't want to argue with him and ruin our evening, I sucked it up and apologized. Something which was hard to do because I didn't really think I was in the wrong. But I knew he was protective over me when it came to other men, so I should have known Cameron wouldn't be any different, family or not.

"Let's not argue about something which isn't even worth discussing." I reached up and grabbed his arm, pulling him to sit down next to me. If I knew anything about the spectacular, mercurial man, it was how to change his mood. He took my offering and sat in the chair to my right. Once seated, he moved his chair closer, his leg brushing against my thigh. Even through the material which separated us, a familiar chill rack my body. He did it to me every single time.

Sensing my reaction, he leaned closer and whispered in my ear, "The look on your face is enough to make me want to hike up your dress and do delicious things to you with my hand." He kissed the shell of my ear. "Would you like that? Would you enjoy my fingers teasing you until you came?" His breath tickled my skin. "Do you want me to make you come in front of everyone here, Sara?"

Where the hell is this coming from? Not two minutes ago he was pissed off and ready to fight his cousin.

He was so damn confusing.

"Behave yourself, Alek," I warned as my nervous fingers played with the decadent gems around my throat. There was genuine consternation in my voice when I addressed him. He wouldn't think twice about following through on his ideas, teasing me unmercifully under the table.

He smiled as his hand disappeared under the tablecloth, hidden from everyone's view. I thought he might have been bluffing until the heat from his hand tickled the top of my thigh. He wasn't looking at me, though. He was engaged in a brief bout of small talk with a gentleman who was sitting opposite us. Every time he made the man chuckle with his wit, the higher his hand would move, closer and closer to my core. Starting to feel a little woozy, I was caught between wanting him to continue and wanting him to curb his teasing. I didn't fully trust myself. But since I didn't know which path to choose, I did nothing, continuing to allow him to set my body on fire.

"I love putting that look on your face, baby," he whispered in my ear again. "But I better stop before there's no going back." He removed his hand from under the table and placed it on his drink.

How the hell am I supposed to concentrate on anything now?

~11~

Alek

After a wonderful dinner, which consisted of way too many rich and decadent foods, I was asked to come up and say a few words to everyone about the night's charity cause. I had my speech all prepared, although with what almost happened with Sara, I needed some time to compose myself. My cock was painfully hard, so much so I didn't stand up right away, willing myself to soften before advancing toward the stage. With the woman sitting next to me, it was almost impossible, but after some time, I was ready.

What the hell was I thinking? I would never really make her come in a room full of people. Her pleasure was for me and me alone. There was no way I would ever allow another man to watch her as she came with my fingers buried deep inside her.

After I rose from the table, I leaned down and gave Sara a quick kiss. Reaching into my pocket, I extracted a piece of paper as I walked toward the stage.

Once situated, I dove right in. "Good evening, everyone. First, let me start off by saying thank you to each and every one of you for coming this evening. Your presence here tonight tells me you support a cause which is dear to my heart. I can't tell you how much your generosity will help those in need of assistance, with those requiring somewhere to go to escape domestic violence. Also for those wishing to just reach out and speak to someone, to ask for guidance, to help fulfill the dream of living in a safe environment.

"We've raised a total of eight hundred and seventy-five thousand dollars tonight. All of the money will go toward a new shelter which is being set up for victims of abuse. Because of all of you, many women and children will have a place to rest their heads, and to be enveloped in a sense of safety. We'll have counselors in-house to help them figure out their next move, a decision which will help them achieve the life they deserve, free from violence and abuse. So thank you again from the bottom of my heart, and please enjoy the rest of your evening."

A thunderous round of applause erupted across the room. I knew it was more for show, but I didn't care. People respected me, and I would take full advantage in order to raise money for the cause. Sure, I could afford to build the shelter myself, had done so many times before, but I wanted others to contribute. I knew everyone in attendance, and it was time they put some of their money to good use.

Once I reached our table, Sara grabbed for my hand and pulled me to sit down next to her again. "Alek, you were great. I can't believe you were able to raise so much money, though. In one single night! How remarkable." She looked astounded, and it was so endearing.

"Well, it was easy enough, seeing as how each dinner cost twenty-five hundred dollars." She blanched at my matter-of-fact statement.

"For one dinner? Wow!"

"I'm happy we had such a great turnout tonight. This is actually the biggest one yet. To know so many more people will be able to obtain the help they need warms my heart."

"You should be proud of yourself. I know I am," she said, her approval meaning more to me than I thought. "But why this cause? Out of all of the causes in the world, what made you hone in on domestic violence? You mentioned it was dear to your heart, but I would love to hear why."

My smile slipped. "That's a conversation best had when we're in private." I saw her disappointment, but there was no way I was going to delve into my past right then. "I would like to tell you the whole story, but I won't do it here."

"Okay, another time then."

"Very soon, Sara. I promise."

~~~~

As the evening wore on, I could see exhaustion starting to take hold of Sara. Actually, I'd started to feel it as well, but I still had people to talk to so I wouldn't be able to leave right away. But I would be quick because I knew her tiredness was going to increase the more time ticked by.

"I have to go and mingle a bit more before we retire for the evening. Would you like to accompany me, or will you be all right by yourself for a short while?"

"No, you go. I'll be fine. Go. Enjoy yourself."

I had to admit I was going to miss her, but the sooner I took care of business, the quicker I could take her home.

"I don't know how much I'll enjoy myself without you by my side, but I'll be quick." I kissed the top of her head as I was pulled away by someone waiting to congratulate me on an eventful evening.

Thirty minutes had passed and I was still no closer to escaping with my woman. I was about to have a conversation with the CEO of a rival company when Jacinda brushed against me. Giving her an annoyed look did nothing to deter her from grabbing my arm and pulling me close. I ignored her. It wasn't the place to cause a scene, and she took advantage of the fact she knew I wasn't going to do or say anything rude to her. Especially not in the presence of the types of people who surrounded us. I wasn't about to fuel unnecessary gossip, so I stood there, the brazen blonde attached to my side.

I ignored her when she ran her fingers up and down my arm. I ignored her when she chimed in on my conversations. I ignored her when she laughed too loudly at jokes which were made in our circle of friends. I even ignored her when she ran her hand over my back.

But when she leaned up and tried to kiss me, I drew the line. Audience or not, there was no way I was going to allow her to continue to be so brazen.

I grabbed her elbow and tried to distance myself from her but she only held firm, doing her best to push closer to me. Since she wasn't going to relent, I let it go.

I'd be having words with her later, though. Plus, I wanted to berate her for talking to Sara the way she had earlier.

There was a lull in the conversation when I decided to try and locate Sara. I hated the fact I'd left her alone at the table with no one to talk to. I knew everyone had basically ignored her. With the exception of Cameron, of course. *He's lucky I didn't punch him right in the face.* Anger returned at the mere thought of him moving close to my woman.

Glancing all around the room, I still hadn't found her. She wasn't sitting at our table. *Maybe she's in the ladies room.* Deciding it had to be where she was, I averted my eyes to focus back on the men in front of me. As I turned my head back toward them, I saw her.

She was at the far end of the bar.

Sitting down.

And she wasn't alone.

My bastard of a cousin was sitting right next to her. Too close. He was way too close to her.

What the fuck? I told her to stay away from him. But again, she chose not to listen to me. Didn't she know I said what I did for her own good?

Appearing rude or not, I excused myself and stealthily walked across the room, my anger building with every heavy step I'd taken. So many things ran through my mind. How upset I was with Sara for not listening to me. How much I wanted to pummel Cameron for even glancing in her direction, let alone touch her in any way. They seemed perfectly cozy together the more I bridged the distance between us.

I'm gonna get arrested tonight. I'm gonna beat the shit out of him, and I'm gonna get arrested.

People stepped in front of me, blocking them from my view. Thankfully, I was able to dismiss them cordially before continuing in my quest to take her away from him. I didn't think I'd ever been so upset before. Trying my best to put the emotion on a leash, I was only ten feet from them when I saw him bump her shoulder with his own.

She laughed.

She laughed and put her hand on his fucking arm.

If I don't calm down, I'm going to give myself a stroke.

They were so engaged in their little conversation, neither one of them saw me approach. Standing directly behind her, my anger bristled within me again, breaking free and rearing its ugly head.

"Are you done?" I seethed, obvious disdain dripping on every word. I was leaning so close to her I knew she felt my breath on her neck.

But I also knew she felt the rage emanating off me. She jumped at my words but never turned around. My eyes shot to Cameron, giving him such a nasty look I was surprised he was still sitting there. If looks could kill, he would have keeled over and ceased to exist. And I wouldn't be sorry. Not for one goddamn second.

I was about to say something else when Sara spoke. "No, actually I am *not* done, Alek. Why don't you go back to letting Jacinda hang all over you, and I'll continue my conversation with Cameron."

What the fuck is she talking about? And how dare she sit there and compare the two. Jacinda was harmless, and I knew how to handle her. Cameron, on the other hand, was a snake. He was predatory and an all-around asshole.

But he wasn't stupid. He and I both knew I could do some real damage if he continued pursuing Sara.

Not even responding to her ludicrous statement, I decided to commandeer the unfolding situation in front of me. "Cameron, I suggest you leave us. Now!" I yelled. I didn't care who saw or heard me. My only objective was getting her alone and away from him.

"It was great talking to you, Sara." He placed his drink on the bar. "See you later," he said as he retreated.

"No, you fucking won't," I threatened through clenched teeth. The bastard actually had the balls to snicker as he walked away. *Oh, just wait until I see you again.*

No longer allowing her to keep her back turned, I grabbed her shoulders and spun her around on her barstool. "Are you out of your mind, Sara? I told you to stay away from him. But of course, you didn't listen." If a person could actually spit nails that would've been the time it would occur.

"We were only talking. I didn't see any harm in conversing with him, especially since you seemed to have your hands full with *that* woman."

"I can't help it if Jacinda was standing near me. What was I supposed to do? Tell her to take a hike, right there in front of everyone? It would have caused an unnecessary scene."

Her face turned red. Clearly she was as heated as I was. "She wasn't *just* standing next to you, Alek, and you know it. She was pawing you, constantly rubbing your arm and acting like you two were together."

"I honestly didn't think anything of it. I'm so used to Jacinda's antics I don't even give her a second thought. Mainly because I couldn't care less about her or what she's doing. I told you repeatedly I'm not interested in her. Not even the tiniest bit."

Sara quickly rose from her chair. We were so close she actually had to look up at me. The look on her face would have been amusing had I not been enraged myself.

"How would you feel if Cameron was constantly touching me? Running his hands all over my body. I have zero interest in him, so would that be acceptable?" She was pushing me over the edge and she knew it.

"I don't even want him looking at you, let alone touching you. So no, Sara, not only is that not acceptable, it's ill-advised. Not unless you want to visit me behind bars."

"Then maybe you should keep that in mind the next time you let her rub against you."

She tried to walk away then, her face becoming more red the longer we argued. Our voices weren't raised, but if anyone paid us any attention they would surely see we were definitely involved in a heated discussion. A lover's quarrel.

I reached for her wrist and pulled her back into me. "Where are you going?"

"Not that it's any of your business, but I'm going to the bathroom. Now, let go of me before *I* cause a scene."

I knew I was being an ass, but my anger hadn't fizzled yet. "Everything you do is my business, Sara. I don't want to argue with you anymore tonight. I've had my say and it's finished."

I abruptly let go of her arm and turned around toward the bartender.

~12~

Sara

How dare he dismiss me the way he did. Who does he think he is?

The whole time I was in the restroom, I tried feverishly to control my emotions. Calm and level-headed were two words that accurately described me. Normally. But whenever Alek twisted me all up inside, I was anything but.

His words kept running through my mind. *"Everything you do is my business, Sara. I don't want to argue with you anymore tonight. I've had my say and it's finished."* The more I repeated them, the angrier I became.

But it wasn't the time or place to discuss it with him. Granted, I didn't listen to him when he told me to stay away from Cameron, but I was a grown woman. I could talk to whomever I wanted, warning or not.

Truth be told, I'd been willing to appease him by steering clear of his cousin, but as soon as I saw how he was acting with Jacinda, or rather how he'd allowed her to act with him, I was livid.

So warnings would be ignored. I sought out Cameron with an agenda.

To make Alek jealous.

To make him feel the same way I did when I saw her rubbing against him.

It worked.

A little too well.

So...did I bring this on myself?

Apparently.

But I'm still not excusing his macho attitude toward me. "I've had my say and it's finished." We'll see about that.

Mumbling to myself about what I should have said in response instead of simply walking away, I washed my hands and headed back out to the ballroom. Most of the people had already left, making it much easier for me to locate the obstinate man I'd come with.

Or so I thought.

Every step I took only reaffirmed how tired I'd become. It'd been a long-ass night. I'd done my best to support Alek, and I figured I'd accomplished what I'd set out to do. But between being ignored most of the night by everyone at the event, being verbally accosted by Jacinda, then getting into an argument with Alek, I was thoroughly exhausted. All I wanted to do was go home, grab a big glass of wine and relax with a long, hot bath before turning in for the evening.

I was willing to let bygones be bygones if he'd just take me home. I'd forgive him his overreaction to Cameron and me chatting. Hell, I'd even forgive him his arrogant comments if he'd simply whisk me away from there.

Searching for Alek, I'd walked around the perimeter of the grand ballroom then made my way through the crowds of remaining people. But I couldn't find him.

When my efforts proved fruitless, I opened my clutch and pulled out my cell. I dialed his number but it went straight to voicemail. *Where the hell is he?*

Before making another round to search for him, I walked outside to take in some fresh air, hoping it would wake me up some. The cool air hit my skin and instantly made me shiver. *Damn, it's chilly out.* Wrapping my arms around myself to save whatever body heat I had left, I paced back and forth in front of the building. When I'd turned around to start in the other direction, I was hit with a sight which made my stomach turn.

My heart sped up.

I'd suddenly become warm.

My anger flared inside me, heating me up until I was ready to blow.

Alek was standing to the far right of the building's entrance, looking as if he was also starved for some fresh air. But he wasn't alone. Jacinda was standing right next to him, her arm resting on his shoulder.

I'd always thought the saying *seeing red* was an exaggeration, but it totally happened. Red specks of rage clouded my vision. They danced in front of me as if beckoning me to take action.

Flabbergasted with the scene unfolding in front of me, I tried to calm myself before I went berserk. The feelings dancing inside me wanted an escape and although I wanted to give in, I knew it was wise to take a step back, take a deep breath and compose myself before I did or said something I'd never be able to take back.

In the midst of trying to calm myself, my eyes never leaving the two of them, I caught her attention. Before I could look away, she leaned up on her tippy toes, wrapped her hands around the back of his neck and pulled him down to meet her lips.

It was as if someone had ripped out my heart and stomped it into a million pieces. My breath escaped me and I'd felt as if I was going to drown in my own hurt if I didn't leave right away.

Luckily, I located his driver with ease, shouting out my address as soon as I approached him. I knew he saw the look in my eye, thankfully never questioning where Alek was.

The whole drive home, I kept the tears at bay, chanting to myself over and over again that I'd deal with whatever happened. *But not tonight. I can't take any more shit tonight.* I yearned for the comfort of my own space, to be surrounded by my things. My solace.

Flicking my phone off was certainly a wise decision because I knew eventually he'd try and call me. He hadn't seen me there, watching the two of them together. For all he knew, I was still inside the event, waiting for him like a dutiful date. And when he finally went back to look for me, I wouldn't be there.

I smiled at the thought of him frantically searching for me, worry and dread surely taking over his features. I knew how much he wanted to keep me safe, a trait which was both sweet and annoying at times. And the mere fact he'd have no idea where I was soothed my anger a little.

We arrived at my place rather quickly. I thanked the driver and practically ran up my front walk, eager to get inside. I was hoping Alexa was out for the evening because I didn't feel like regaling my night's experience with her. Not yet, at least. I was way too exhausted to even entertain my own thoughts, let alone explain everything in detail to someone else.

I made my way to the bathroom and started running a nice, hot bubble bath. While I was waiting for the tub to fill, I headed to the kitchen to grab some wine. Forget the glass, I took the whole bottle with me, taking a big swig before I even made it to my bedroom to undress.

Once my bath was ready, I lowered myself in gently, already feeling the night's escapades slipping away. I drank quite a bit more of the

chilled wine before closing my eyes and letting the water work its
magic on my tense limbs.

I had no clue as to how much time had passed, but it must have been
significant because the water started to cool. As I raised my upper
body to lean forward and turn the faucet back on, I heard someone
yelling for me, the voice moving closer and closer to my bathroom
door. Before I could move a single inch, the door came crashing open,
hitting the wall behind it with an unexpected force.

Note to self: Ask for his set of my keys back.

"Jesus Christ, Sara!" Alek shouted. "I didn't know what the hell
happened to you. Why didn't you tell me you were leaving? I must
have called you like a thousand times." He was quite the sight,
deserving every bit of his disheveled state. "I searched everywhere for
you. It wasn't until I talked to my driver that I found out he'd given
you a ride home." He paced back and forth in front of the vanity,
shoving his hands through his already ruffled hair.

The only thing I could do was watch him. Even in his disgruntled
state, he was the most handsome man I'd ever seen. *Stop thinking this
shit. Be angry. Be adamant. But don't be horny.*

No words escaped me. Even if I'd wanted to respond, I wouldn't
even know where to begin. He'd surprised me by not only bursting
into my apartment but into my bathroom as well, disrupting the only
peace I'd been able to achieve in the past few hours.

My silence was apparently the wrong choice.

"Well? Are you going to answer me or what?" Concern and anger dueled behind his eyes. I knew I'd scared him, but he deserved it, so I wasn't going to apologize for my disappearance.

"I turned my phone off because I didn't want to speak to you. And I'm not going to discuss this any further with you, especially while I'm naked in the tub and you're looming over me in that domineering way of yours."

"We *are* going to finish this, so dry off and get dressed, or don't. It's up to you. I'll be waiting in the living room." He stomped off without waiting for me to reply, which didn't really shock me at all. Surprisingly.

Grabbing my towel from the rack, I dried off as quickly as possible and made my way to my room to find some clothes. I wasn't going to rush around like a crazy lady simply because he was pissed and wanted to finish our conversation. I deliberately took my time dressing, donning shorts and a comfy T-shirt.

My lack of quickness had Alek looming in my doorway, his hands shoved into the pockets of his tuxedo pants. His presence took up the entire space, making me feel much smaller. His tie was all but ripped off, hanging to the side as if he'd wrestled with it in anger.

"What's taking you so long?" he barked. "The longer you make me wait, the more pissed off I am."

"Well, I don't give a shit if you're mad, Alek. I'm the only one here who's allowed to be pissed off, so just...back off!" My own anger spewed forth, completely out of my control. I'd thought I'd calmed down, but all he had to do was show up and start shouting and it came back full-force.

"Why are *you* so upset? What happened?"

I shook my head in wonderment. He really was dense sometimes, or at least he faked it well enough.

"Well, let's see. First, you totally disregarded my argument about Jacinda, blowing my concerns off, as usual. Then, I caught you kissing her outside the hotel. Does that explain it enough for you?" My own fists clenched at my sides, oddly mirroring him to a tee.

His face instantly changed, his eyes becoming bigger with each word escaping my lips.

"It's not what you think," he all but whispered.

"Yeah...it never is, is it, Alek?" I couldn't control the sarcasm which dripped off every word.

"She kissed me. I didn't kiss her. And as soon as she pulled her little stunt, I pushed her off me and instantly walked away from her. Did you even stick around long enough to see that part?" He stepped closer. "Did you?"

"It doesn't matter who kissed who, Alek." It *did* matter, but I wasn't going to let him off the hook. I did witness her make the first move, but he should've never been with her in the first place. None of it would've happened if he'd taken into account how I felt about her. "I don't want to talk about this anymore. I want you to go."

"No. I'm not leaving until this is resolved. I didn't do anything wrong here. I didn't kiss her, and I think you know it. I have no interest in her at—"

I cut him off before he finished his repetitive statement. "Yeah, you keep telling me you have no interest in her. Yet, every time I turned around tonight, she was somehow right next to you. Why is that?"

"I don't know, honestly. I've told her repeatedly I don't have any romantic feelings for her. And she seemed to be okay with it. Well, until she kissed me, that is."

My last ounce of emotional reserve had finally depleted. I became upset again, but it wasn't in anger. The truth was, he hurt me.

Tears welled behind my eyes, and even though I didn't want them to explode, they did. And there wasn't a damn thing I could do about it. Not anymore.

Both physically and mentally drained, I had to release everything inside me before it ate me up.

"Can you please just go?" I said through my tears, hiccupping between words because I was so upset. "I don't want to talk anymore tonight." I tried to shove him from my room, but he wouldn't budge. Not one inch. Instead, he tried to reach for me, instantly causing me to back up.

"Sara, please. Please, come here. I'm sorry." He continued to walk toward me and when I had nowhere left to escape, I fell on top of my bed. He lowered himself until our faces were only inches apart. I tried with all of my remaining strength to push him off me, but it was of no use. "Baby. I'm so sorry. Please...please, don't cry. I never want to hurt you. From now on, I promise I'll stay away from her. I won't put myself in that position again. I underestimated her feelings for me and I'm sorry. I can't apologize enough. Please, forgive me."

When I said nothing, he leaned in closer and kissed me. His lips were soft yet pleading. He was asking for my trust and forgiveness. For so many things. His mouth lingered on mine until my lips parted, an action which caused him to seize the opportunity to deepen our entanglement. He expertly seized my mouth but before things went too far, I swiftly broke the kiss, turning my head to the side so I wouldn't lose myself in him any further.

Moments later, he leaned up and kissed my forehead, finally pushing himself off the bed.

"I'll go for now. I don't want to make you any more upset than you already are. Again, I'm truly sorry." He didn't make a move to leave. I figured he was waiting for me to say something, anything to let him know we would be okay.

I gave him what he was looking for.

"I'll talk to you tomorrow. Goodnight."

My words allowed him to leave my room although he was clearly distraught, not being able to swoop in and fix the very same mess he'd created.

~13~

Sara

It took me a whole day to finally calm down, the pain Alek caused needing time to slowly fade. I knew in my heart he would never hurt me on purpose, but it still took my head more time to come to the same realization.

He'd apologized profusely, promising to never let anything like that happen again. I believed him. Maybe it was foolish, but I did nonetheless.

A whole week had gone by since I last laid eyes on him. We had talked every day, sometimes multiple times. But between me needing some time to deal with everything, being busy at work and him being away on business, we hadn't been able to slice out some time to be together.

Our sexual frustration was reaching an all-time high, sometimes manifesting by becoming easily aggravated with one another on the phone.

It was early morning when he called. Sunday was my one free day of the week, so I'd been anticipating us being able to do something together.

"Hey, beautiful." He sounded in a good mood.

"Hi, babe. Please, tell me you're calling to whisk me away." I hoped his call wasn't merely another check-in. I missed him. My body missed him, and I didn't know how much more I could take. I was starving for his touch and I hoped he felt the same way.

"Yes, I am. I'll be there in forty-five minutes. Enough is enough already. I can't stand not seeing you, holding you, being buried deep inside you." His tone dipped into a sexy gravel toward the end of his declaration.

He literally made me squirm around on my bed. Excitement was filling the air, and I wanted him to continue.

It was the first time either one of us had even referenced having sex again. Sure, there were small comments here and there, but nothing significant. But I was ready. He was right. Enough was enough. *What the hell am I holding out for?*

"You want to be buried deep inside me, do you? What else do you want to do to me, Alek? Huh?" My own tone was much more breathy than normal and I heard him falter on the other end, waiting what seemed like forever before he responded.

"I'm not wasting precious minutes describing what I want to do to you over the phone. I'll be more than happy to show you in person. I'll be there in half an hour."

"I thought you said forty-five minutes." I tried not to laugh, but I could tell he was worked up and would probably break all traffic laws just to reach me.

"Well, that was before you asked me what else I wanted to do to you. You better be ready for me when I arrive, baby, because I'm going to make you beg and scream."

Then all I heard was dead air.

~~~~

In preparation for his arrival, I took a quick shower, shaved all necessary areas, brushed my teeth and made sure my long, dark hair cascaded down my back in nice, big waves. *He needs something to grab on to, right?*

Instead of getting dressed, I pulled on a short, red silk robe and waited until I heard his car.

Once I knew he was outside, I moved toward my front door and opened it as he was approaching. As soon as he saw me, he gifted me with one of his panty-dropping smiles. If I wasn't afraid of anyone hearing, I would have jumped him right there in the hallway.

He was two steps in to my apartment when he pulled me close. Reaching down with both arms, he grabbed me underneath my backside and raised me up. Without any instruction, my legs wrapped around his waist, and it was then he noticed I was naked underneath my robe.

"I'm going to fuck you so hard, baby. I've missed you too much." His lips were on me before he took another step.

"We have to be quiet because Alexa is actually home for once," I announced, my fingers weaving through his thick hair.

"Then she's going to hear us because there is no way we're being quiet. I've waited way too long for this, and I don't care who's around."

Every step toward my bedroom was sweet torture. His kiss told of his frustrated need for me. I only hoped I'd told the same tale with mine. He gripped me closer as if he was afraid I'd disappear. My body was on fire, and instinct told me he was going to draw out our time together until I was indeed begging and screaming for him to fuck me senseless.

His fingers danced over my flesh as I held him tight, weaving his desire for me into every pore of my skin. Just when I couldn't take anymore, we breached the entryway to my bedroom.

Once inside, he closed the door behind him and released his hold on me, allowing me to slide down his body until my feet hit the ground.

Pushing me against the nearest wall, he slammed his mouth to mine, his tongue taking over, trying to claim as much of me as he could. A small moan tumbled forth, prompting him to grind his rock-hard arousal into my belly.

My flimsy robe must have annoyed him, the left side of the material falling over my breast and hiding me from him. He quickly pushed it off my shoulders until it broke free and fell to the ground at my feet.

His gaze flitted over me, starting with my eyes, stopping for a few seconds too long on my lips, then cascading down the length of the rest of my body.

Squirming under his intense gaze did nothing but spur his visual assault further. The longer he admired me the needier I became. It wasn't fair. He was still fully clothed, shielding his amazing physique from my eyes.

As I was about to protest, he spoke.

"Goddamn it," he groaned. "It's been way too long." After another minute of him just staring at me, he broke the building tension only to utter five words which threw me into another world. "You make me feel helpless."

What the hell does he mean? Helpless? If anyone was helpless, it was me. But I didn't have any time to explore his outburst before he made his demands.

~14~

Sara

"I want your mouth on me, Sara. Now." He sure as hell didn't need to tell me twice.

Lowering myself until my knees hit the soft plushness of the carpet, I reached out and grabbed his belt, pulling him toward me as I whipped it through the loops in one fluid movement. Once the leather was free, I popped the top button of his jeans, slowly dragging the zipper down until his pants were completely free from restraint. Hooking my fingers in the waistband, I lowered them down his strong, sculpted legs, taking his black boxer briefs with them, until he was gloriously naked from the waist down. His cock sprang free and hit his abdomen. He grunted when my hands reached around and gripped his hard, perfect ass, pulling him closer to my mouth.

I was close enough to taste him, so I didn't waste any precious time. My tongue darted out and gently made contact, running from the base all the way up to his swollen tip.

"Like that?" I asked seductively. "Is that what you want me to do?" I didn't even give him a chance to respond before I took him into the warmth of my mouth, swirling my tongue around and teasing him unmercifully.

"Fuck, baby, you're gonna be the death of me. Your mouth feels amazing." He braced himself against the wall with both arms, towering over my crouching form. "Take me all the way. I want to feel the back of your throat." He was doing his best to control himself, which was all the more reason for me to tempt and tease him. Pleasure him until he shouted from his release. It had become my main goal.

With every flick of my tongue, he grunted and groaned, thrusting his hips forward, trying to move deeper into my mouth. Luckily for him I didn't have a sensitive gag reflex.

I slipped my lips further and further down his shaft, teasing him the whole way, licking and nipping at his crown before devouring the rest of him. I released my grip from his firm backside only to grab hold of the base of his cock. I started stroking him up and down, my hand mimicking and accompanying my mouth. It was slow at first, but the more his body twitched, the quicker my movements became. I found my rhythm rather swiftly. When I raised my head slightly to look at him, his eyes were on me, watching me pleasure him. Watching my cheeks sink in as I sucked him hard. Watching my hand as I stroked him.

His mouth was slightly agape, his lids heavy with desire as he crested toward his release. His tongue ran over his bottom lip, and it was that action which spurred my assault even more.

He lowered his arm from the wall and grabbed the back of my hair, pushing himself even further inside. "Fuck, Sara!" he exclaimed. "I can't get enough of your beautiful mouth." A fierce moan escaped from deep within him. He circled his hips, gently at first, but the more he was affected, the faster his gyrations became. He was close, and even though I'd never performed the act before, I knew what came next.

Alexa had made me sit through countless movies, trying her best to prepare me for when the time came. *What are best friends for, after all?*

There was no doubt in my mind I wanted to taste Alek. I meant *really* taste him. Anything he was willing to give me would be accepted with a big smile on my face. I loved the way he made my inhibitions disappear.

"Damn it...I'm gonna come!" he roared. "Fuck...I'm gonna explode. If you don't want to swallow, pull back now!"

His words only made me greedier. I wanted his hot, salty liquid to fill my mouth. I wanted to taste him and take everything from him.

To know I'd brought him such pleasure was a powerful feeling. I kept one hand on the base of his shaft, coaxing his orgasm from him, and lifted my free hand so it rested on the distinguishable part of the

V which graced his lower abdomen. I let loose and sucked him so hard, he finally let go and climaxed.

His explosion hit the back of my throat and I swallowed it all. I continued to milk every single drop from him until he was completely spent.

When he was finally done, he reached down and pulled me up so I was trapped between him and the wall behind me. He was still trying to regulate his breathing, my assault on him literally leaving him breathless.

I locked eyes with him, winked and then smiled, innocently asking, "Did you like that?"

"I fucking loved it, baby. I wasn't too rough, though, was I? For as much as I pride myself on my restraint, I always seem to lose control when it comes to you."

"Not at all. And just so you know, I love when you lose control with me." My need to pleasure him was so overwhelming, I would do whatever he wanted. Whatever he needed.

Grabbing my chin, he raised it until his lips found me again. He enraptured me, tasting remnants of his own release on my tongue. Kicking his jeans the rest of the way off, he pulled his shirt over his head and briskly walked us over to my bed. He bent down and picked me up only to toss me through the air. I screamed from the surprise but laughed immediately when I hit the middle of the massive bed.

"Now it's my turn to make you scream." He pushed my legs apart. "Show me where you want me to kiss you. Show me with your hands. Point to where you want my mouth." My head was thrown back on the bed, but I didn't need to see in order to tell him where I wanted pleasure. I did as he said and showed him with my hands. I initially pointed between my legs, first near my knees then slowly moving up until I reached the apex of my thighs.

He graced me with his beautiful mouth, ravaging every part of me shown to him. He was licking, sucking and biting his way up my body toward where he really wanted to go. But he was taking his instructions from me, not moving up further until I gave him permission. Then finally, after I couldn't bear it any longer, I put my hand over my sex. I knew I was hot and slick to the touch. And it was all because of him and his beautifully skilled mouth.

He reached my hand's current position. "Right here? Is this where you want me to kiss you? Tell me," he demanded. I could only hum my response, words totally escaping me. "I want to hear you tell me. I want you to say the words or I'm not going any further." His warm breath touched my most intimate of places, driving me crazy. I flexed my hips, pushing myself closer to him, enticing him to take the bait. But he wouldn't. "Tell me now, Sara!" he warned.

"Yes."

"Yes what?" He loved the power he had over me. It was too obvious.

"Please...kiss me here."

Moving my fingers out of the way, his mouth descended onto me. Starting off with one long lick, striking between my swollen folds. "You're so wet. Is that all for me?"

"Yes, always for you," I panted. I knew better than to not answer him. I didn't want him to stop and hold out on me.

Switching tempos was his specialty. He would start off slow, really enjoying the teasing dance he orchestrated. Then as I fell into his trap, he would devour me quickly, causing me to match his rhythm with my hips.

He would go in intervals, making me enjoy every bit of his domination over my body. Engulfing my desire with each flick of his tongue.

He knew when I was close because my breathing became ragged and uncontrollable moans would escape. Too many for me to count. He played my body like an instrument, coaxing every bit of desire from me. When he knew I was about to let go, he pushed a skillful finger inside me, making me squirm and suck in the air around me.

It didn't take long before detonation was staring me down. "Oh, God, Alek, I'm gonna come. I'm gonna come!" I shouted as I writhed under his touch.

"In that case..." He withdrew his hand completely, only to thrust two fingers back inside me, adding his mouth over my hypersensitive clit.

I grabbed the sheets with both fists, making my knuckles turn white from the gripping pressure. I spread my legs wider and thrust up toward his mouth, jerking wildly on the bed.

"Alek...oh, God...Alek." I was lost in delirium. I couldn't control my own body, and it was a little scary. It was frightening what he could do to me with his touch. I was powerless under him, and I knew I always would be.

"Let it go. Come now!" I had no choice but to give in to his expert touch. My body convulsed with pure pleasure, the waves of my orgasm racking through my body, threatening to never stop.

It was almost as if I was floating above myself, experiencing such an intense level of pleasure.

When he detected I was coming back down, he slowed his tongue's strokes on my body, allowing me to relish in the aftermath of my explosion. He withdrew his fingers from inside me only after I had completely relaxed into his touch.

Not wasting another precious second, he made his way up the bed. It was his turn to wink and smile at me, and I laughed.

"We were made for each other. Do you know that? Do you feel it here?" He placed his hand back over where his mouth just was. "And do you feel it here?" He raised his hand to cover my heart. "I've waited for you for what seems like an eternity. Just going through life's daily motions. Biding my time." I saw the sincerity in his piercing gaze and felt it in his sweet, loving kiss. Every time our mouths met it was electric, like something you only read about. I didn't know a connection like ours could really exist between two people, let alone exist for me.

Not knowing what to say in response, I simply tangled my fingers in his hair and pulled him close, expressing myself through my kiss. It seemed to please him.

We both attempted to stake a claim on the other, trying to show each other what we felt, all wrapped up in demanding tongues and bruised lips. Alek released both of my hands from his dark strands and pinned them above my head, holding them together with one grip. He nudged my thighs apart with his strong leg and pushed his replenished arousal in between, grinding in circular motions. He moved his scrumptious lips from my mouth to my ear, releasing a deep moan which made me struggle against him. I wanted so badly to feel him, to wrap my arms around him, but he wasn't having any of it.

~15~

Alek

"You want to touch me, don't you?" I hummed into her ear. "Well, you can't. Not yet. The only thing I'm going to allow you to feel is my thick cock buried deep inside you." My mouth moved slowly toward her shoulder, biting at her fiery flesh.

Teasing her was my new favorite thing to do. Although, judging from her frustrated movements, she wasn't too appreciative. Thrusting her hips upward, her impatience eating away at her, she thought she could hurry along my need to take her. But she was wrong. So wrong. Even though it'd seemed like ages since the last time I was inside her, I was going to take my time. Work her up so good she would lose all sense of what she wanted. No...what she *needed*.

Wrapping her gorgeous thighs around my waist almost undid me.

Almost.

"Don't make me wait. Please," she pleaded. She had wanted to take things slowly since she'd given me another chance and I didn't push her, knowing she needed the time. But hearing her beg for me was the best feeling. Well...not the *best* feeling, but pretty close.

She was rendered a shameless pool of desire but for some reason, I doubted she cared. Not one single bit.

"Now is as good a time as any for me to practice self-control, don't you think?" I asked, knowing full well she was becoming even more frustrated the longer I waited.

She groaned into my neck, her warm breath tickling my skin.

I was waiting her out, her submission was the ultimate goal. I wasn't going to tell her in words, but rather in actions. She would catch on eventually. I had faith in her.

Thankfully, she finally relented. Halting all movement to try and tempt me further, she expelled a quick rush of air and laid still. Her eyes never left my face, and it was in those pools of beautiful amber that I saw her offer to me.

"Good girl," I teased. "You know I'm the one in charge in here, right?"

She nodded. One simple gesture, but it was all I was looking for.

Deciding my own teasing was driving me nuts as well, I leaned in closer, trying my best to capture her mouth. I needed to feel her sweet breath against my lips. I needed her tongue to dance with mine. I simply needed to taste her.

As I was about to close the distance between us, she quickly moved her head to the side. Figuring she wanted me to kiss her neck, I complied. Her pulse beat faster the more my lips teased her skin. Soon, I tried to kiss her again, and again she turned her head to the side. She thought she was being slick. She thought I hadn't caught on to what she was doing. But she was wrong.

She was trying to tease me in return. Punish me for what I'd been doing to her for the past fifteen minutes.

I hated being denied her touch. I'd held fast to my restraint before but right then, her lying naked beneath me, I couldn't hold back any longer. "What are you playing at, Sara? Kiss me, damn it!" I commanded. My aggravation must have been amusing to her because the only thing she did was smile at me. While she was even more beautiful in that moment, she was also dangerously close to being tortured. I would do things to her body, bring her so close to falling but pull back right at the last minute. Over and over again.

I tried one more time. Intensifying my hold on her arms above her head, I went in for the kill.

Again she refused my need for her.

I was done. No more games. I wouldn't tolerate her refusal any longer. It was time I voiced what I had planned for her if she denied me again.

Before I could speak, she tried her best to plead her case. "You're not giving me what I want, Alek, so I'm not giving you what you want." She turned her head to the side and held the air in her lungs, not really sure what my reaction would be to her continued insolence.

"Is that right?" My tone was brazen, full of cockiness. "If you have any hope of me taking you tonight, you better kiss me, woman. If you deny me one more time, I'll tie you up, tease you relentlessly but make sure to stop each and every time you're about to come." I grabbed her chin with my free hand and turned her face so she could stare into my eyes. "Just try me."

I was dead serious; my gaze said as much. I cocked a brow and waited for her obedience. "Let's try this again," I said before slowly lowering my mouth to hers, purposely taking my time. I was doing my best to try and give her those couple of extra seconds to contemplate the consequences if she decided to refuse me again.

I was sure she thought she was only playing with me. What she didn't understand was her denial hit me hard. I took it personally, and although I did my best to play along with her little game, it was over.

I hovered above her, holding my position. I not only wanted her to accept me, I wanted her to be the one to make the first contact. I knew I was being an ass, but it worked. She lifted her head from the pillow and pressed her swollen lips to mine. When her tongue left her mouth and entangled with mine, she took the opportunity to exact her revenge. She sunk her teeth in, softly but with enough pressure for me to react.

"Ow." I backed up and glared at her. *Good for her.*

"What? I thought you liked that," she said, feigning innocence. I knew her actions were done on purpose, but my facial expression never gave it away.

"Uh-huh," I mumbled. She laughed, but when I took possession of her mouth again, I did the same thing to her. It shocked her at first, mirroring my own reaction, but instead of resisting, she gave in to me.

Hearing the soft sounds of the clock over the bed only drove home our time together was slowly slipping away. I had to make our reunion count. Wasting no more frivolous time, I parted her thighs with my leg, my grip still pinning her arms above her head. I wasn't ready to let her touch me yet. Call it my last-ditch effort to punish her for refusing my kiss.

Reaching down, I ran my hand through her pussy, her desire coating the tip of my fingers. She was wetter than before, her need betraying her willpower from earlier.

Gripping my thick length, I lined myself up, prepared to claim her once and for all. "Are you ready for me, baby?" I asked, knowing full well she was.

She tried to free her hands, desperate to touch me, claw at me and pull me closer. Once inside, I would release her, both emotionally and physically.

I knew she'd been struggling as much as I had been, if not more, since I'd revealed my secret to her. We both feared what we'd shared together was nothing more than a farce, even though I knew better. It merely took her longer to come to the same conclusion, that we were destined to be with each other.

I'd known it from the first time I'd laid eyes on her photo.

She'd known it the first time her eyes connected with mine.

I'd be forever grateful to Fate that she picked my city to move to. A random act, but one which finally brought us together.

I repeated my question since she seemed to be at a loss for words. The only way she'd responded was by writhing around underneath me. Her lips were red and bruised from my kiss, her cheeks flushed with her desire for me to finally take her. "Are you ready for me?" I asked her again.

"Don't make me wait any longer. What you're doing right now is torture. Please..." she begged. One lone tear escaped and danced down her cheek. It was enough to break me.

Knowing it had been a little while since we last had sex, I made sure to not take her as roughly as I wanted. I had to be gentle. I had to practice control, keep my wants on a leash until I deemed it safe.

Pushing into her tight heat did everything to unravel me. I'd never felt more at home than when I was inside her, our bodies joining in utter bliss.

Freeing her hands, she quickly clutched my back as we rocked together. Sweat glistened on her skin the more excited she became. A lock of hair fell over my eye, its annoyance too much because the strands blocked her from my view, if only partially. She fixed me immediately. Her fingers pushed my hair back, tangling my tresses in her grasp the closer she came to her release.

"Alek..." she cried, her pleasure almost unbearable.

"Are you going to come, sweetheart?"

"Yes. Fuck me harder. Please."

Sara was not someone who swore on a regular basis. But when she did, especially in the bedroom, it was like music to my ears. Far be it from me not to give her what she wanted, especially when she asked me so nicely.

Reaching underneath her, I rested my hand on the small of her back and changed positions until I was resting on my knees, her body slightly in the air for a better position.

If she wants harder, I'll give her harder.

Gripping her waist, I fucked her with wild abandon. Her cries told me she loved it. Her whimpers sang out she was close.

"Wait for me, Sara. Don't come without me," I demanded. The look in her eyes revealed she was struggling with not letting her body release the ecstasy she was desperately holding on to. I felt for her, really I did. But I wanted to release myself inside her at the same time her walls clamped down on my cock.

Desire washing over each other, need licked at our very core.

"I can't stop it. I can't..." she implored. "Please, come with me now."

Two more deep thrusts and my body convulsed. There were no words spoken between us. She saw in my gaze I was unravelling.

As did she.

All over me.

Her nails dug into my skin on the last wave of her explosion. The feelings washing over me were too much and I welcomed the bite of pain she gifted me.

~16~

Alek

As we lay there in our blissful aftermath, a thought occurred to me. One which would have had me upset months before. But now...the thought was almost comforting.

In my haste to claim my woman, I'd forgotten to put on a condom. As my seed ran down her inner thigh, I couldn't help but think how thrilled I would be if our union, or *reunion*, led to her becoming pregnant.

We'd never discussed the possibility before, the topic never leaving either one of our lips. But the thought of her swollen with my child was more pleasant than not. I knew it wasn't the way I would have chosen to do things, but I couldn't change anything.

What's done is done.

No going back.

I should let her in on what was going on. "Sara," I whispered, pulling her close to snuggle in to me. "Don't freak out, but...uh...we forgot to use a condom." It was a real shame I had to destroy her peaceful world, but I didn't have a choice. I had to voice the obvious and let her come around slowly instead of her realizing it on her own when she went to wash up.

I trailed my fingertips down her belly, slowly moving toward her pussy. I wanted to feel my essence one more time before the realization of what I'd just told her hit her hard. *Maybe if I tease her, bring her more pleasure, she won't freak out.*

You think if you give her another orgasm she'll overlook the fact she could end up pregnant? Because you weren't responsible enough to remember to wrap it up?

Delusional.

As I was about to circle her clit with my thumb, she shot off the bed.

"Please tell me you're joking, Alek," she cried. "I'm not on the pill."

She shook her head so fast, as if her movements alone would rid her of her current circumstance. "No, no, no," she repeated, her hands gripping her long hair in frustration. "This can't be happening." She stopped her tirade and suddenly locked eyes on me. "I don't want children. Ever," she forcefully declared.

Granted, I knew she would react to the fact we hadn't used protection, but the more she went on the more I started to feel...offended? Not even sure if that was the right word or not, I jumped off the bed and closed the distance between us. Holding out my hands, I tried to beckon her to me, but she wasn't having any of it.

In fact, she backed up, looking more like a wounded animal than a woman caught in an unpredictable situation.

"Don't," she whispered, taking another step back.

My face fell. I knew she was worried, scared even, but there was no reason for her to react in such a way.

"Sara, come here." She moved further away. "Sara," I called. "Come. Here."

Fight or flight.

She was certainly ready for flight.

I caught her wrist as she was about to bolt into the bathroom. The fact she was completely naked did nothing to detract from how frightened she was.

The mere look in her eye told me she needed a minute alone. I let go of her hand and she ran into the bathroom, slamming and locking the door behind her.

I knew most women wouldn't wish for their lives to change without their utmost planning, but she had to know I'd be happy and would be there for her one hundred percent. She'd never have to worry about expenses, or healthcare or any of the other worries which plague women.

If she even ended up pregnant.

There was a huge chance nothing would happen. I'd never gotten a woman pregnant before. Hell, I could be sterile for all I knew.

You've always used a condom before, jackass. Don't be so dramatic.

During the midst of our argument, I'd heard the front door open and close. Our *disagreement* had obviously forced Alexa to give us some privacy.

Muffled cries sounded from inside the bathroom. I knew I had to try to persuade her to come out, or at least open the door so we could speak.

"Sara. Baby. Please don't be upset, honey. We'll work through whatever happens. I'm here for you, sweetheart. I love you."

I chose then to express my feelings for her yet again because it was what she needed to hear. Hell, it was what I needed to say. I wanted her to remember I wasn't going anywhere, that I did, in fact, love her and was only too happy to speak those three words out loud.

The door whipped open so fast I had to take a quick step back. "If you really loved me, you wouldn't have put me in this predicament," she yelled.

"Is the mere thought of carrying my child that frightening?" I asked, trying my best to convince her to talk to me instead of putting distance between us. "I know we've never discussed having children, but you act as if it would be the worst thing to bring my baby into this world."

She remained silent, her face warring between being angry and panicked. Minutes passed with us simply staring at each other, no closer to ending our argument. *Is this even a fight?*

Reaching down, I gathered my clothes. Not wanting to do or say anything I'd regret later on, I decided it was best for me to leave.

She bridged the gap between us, reaching out to touch my arm. Her face was suddenly calmer, her breathing not as erratic. "Please, don't leave," she said. "It's not all your fault. I'm just as responsible in this. I...I just...I don't know," she confessed, looking more confused than before.

I wasn't going to lie and say her reaction didn't hurt me, but she'd stolen my heart when she'd started to cry.

Gathering her in my embrace, I kissed the top of her head. "What's the matter? Why are you so upset? You can tell me." I pushed her away from me so I could look into her face. Her anger had disappeared, but worry and fear shone bright.

After taking a deep breath, she relaxed in my hold. "I didn't mean to offend you, Alek. In another life, I would be ecstatic to have your children. But in this life...it's just not possible."

"I don't understand," I implored. "Why?"

Taking another deep breath, she revealed her reasoning. "I could never bring a child into this world knowing there are people like Samuel out there. Too many of them," she whispered.

I was shocked she even mentioned *his* name, making any reference at all as to what had happened to her all those years before. She didn't talk about it and I never pushed her, so for her to speak in such a way told me how truly frightened she was.

"Baby, I would never let anyone hurt our child. You have to believe me."

"You can't protect them from the evils of the world." She tried to break free from my embrace but I held firm. "Something terrible will happen, and I would never be able to live through it. I barely lived through what I suffered. It nearly killed my grandmother. No," she said, shaking her head. "I won't do it. I can't."

Her fears were irrational to me, but they made sense to her. And I understood. *For now.*

I kissed her again and did my best to calm her down.

It killed me that I couldn't protect Sara from her fears. I'd vowed so long ago to keep an eye on her and I'd made good on my promise. But being in a relationship with her was even more trying because I couldn't protect what ran rampant inside her head.

I did my best to quell her delusions, but I knew it wasn't enough.

Not yet.

~17~

Sara

Two weeks.

It'd been two weeks since the last time we had sex, and didn't use a condom. Two weeks since my emotional breakdown.

I apologized to Alek several times, and each time he told me to stop being so hard on myself. He understood my outburst, but I knew I'd still hurt him. Offended him, even.

If I were a different woman, I'd jump at the opportunity to have babies with him. But I wasn't. I was me, and I never planned on bringing life into the world.

Based on last month's cycle, I should have gotten my period two days ago. But they had never been regular before, so I was doing my best not to freak out.

For as much as I'd wanted to take a test the day after we had sex, I knew I was being irrational. There was no way to tell so early.

So I'd waited.

Fourteen days.

I finally decided to stop by a drug store and pick up a pregnancy test. I chose the one in the purple box. They all looked the same to me, so it didn't really matter.

Alek had asked if he could be there with me when I found out, good or bad, but I told him I needed to do it alone. If it was bad news, I would need time to process it and if it was good news, I didn't want to subject him to my giddiness. I'd never imagined he even considered the possibility of having children with me. The thought was so touching yet scared the shit out of me.

Once home, I went straight into the bathroom and opened the box. Reading the instructions did nothing but delay the inevitable. Sitting down on the toilet, I proceeded to pee on the stick, praying the entire time I wasn't with child.

Five minutes was all the box said it would take to find out. A minus sign was negative and a plus sign was positive.

Come on minus sign.

Ten minutes passed and still I didn't look. I left the test on the sink counter and headed toward my bedroom, wanting nothing more than to escape the confines of the tiny washroom.

"Sara," Alexa called out as she entered our apartment. "Are you here?"

Shit! I hadn't told her anything about what happened. I figured if I didn't talk about it...it wasn't real.

I quickly tried to make my way toward the bathroom to hide the evidence, but she beat me to it. She was staring at my future, resting on the lip of the countertop.

Turning her head in my direction, she whispered, "What is that?" She knew damn well what it was, but she wanted me to confirm it.

"It's a pregnancy test."

"Are you?" She moved closer and grabbed my hand for support. She had no idea how much I'd needed her small gesture.

"I don't know. I haven't checked it yet."

"Do you want me to look for you?" she asked as she took a step across the threshold of the bathroom, her eyes never leaving mine for fear I would crumble to the floor.

I simply nodded.

She grabbed hold of the directions and read them quickly before picking up the stick. The corners of her mouth curved up to form the smallest of smiles. Her expression could mean she was happy I was going to have a little one running around, or it could mean she was happy not to have to put up with a screaming child waking her up in the middle of the night.

Slowly, she turned around and faced me. It was mere seconds before I found out what her smile truly meant.

"You're not pregnant."

I exhaled a rush of air and closed my eyes. *Thank God.* As I moved toward my best friend to grab the stick to see for myself, a few tears escaped. The funny thing was I had no idea if I was happy or sad.

Damn Alek for confusing me. Damn him for his undying support and his promise to keep our potential child safe. I knew he would make good on his promise, too.

Deciding not to dwell on thoughts I didn't completely understand yet, my eyes focused on the dash which appeared in the tiny window of the pregnancy test.

Yep, I'm not pregnant.

Now all I have to do is tell Alek.

~18~

Alek

My reaction to the results of Sara's pregnancy test was controlled. I knew how she felt about the whole situation, so I tried to reel in my disappointment at the news. There was plenty of time to persuade her to reconsider in the future.

I couldn't believe I was looking forward to discussing the possibility of starting a family with anyone. But Sara wasn't just any woman. She was the love of my life and I knew it. I knew it deep inside my soul.

As the weeks passed, we had long talks about our relationship and where we saw things going. Sometimes I acted as if I was the woman, wanting to know where we stood. I held back most times, but inside my head, I was a fucking nightmare. *I* wanted to punch me.

~~~~

One afternoon, I asked her to join me on a little shopping excursion, needing to pick up some new things for my office. As I knew she would, she agreed.

Our day together was relaxing. We were having a blast, reveling in each other's company. No stress. She wasn't prompting me to make any crazy demands, and therefore I didn't have to deal with her stubbornness. I managed to remain calm and free-spirited all day. It was a side of me I knew she liked seeing.

"I wish every day could be like this, so carefree and jovial." Her tone was hopeful.

"If you would listen to me and do as I ask then every day *could* be this nice." The grin on my face told her everything. I was indeed making light of my crazy statement.

"Yeah, well, that'll never happen, so we may as well enjoy the moment," she said, giving me her best smirk. While the majority of our time spent together was happy and blissful, there were times we argued. Not full-on fighting, just disagreeing. She pushed my buttons, as I did hers. We would bicker then would be done with it, nine times out of ten ending up in bed, fucking each other senseless.

We were walking hand in hand in front of the many little shops in the center of town when I heard someone call out my name. Looking ahead, I couldn't see who it was until a man parted through the small crowd.

Glancing at Sara, I couldn't help the huge ear-splitting grin which spread across my surprised face.

"Devera? Is that you?" he shouted as he quickened his pace.

Ushering Sara forward, I bridged the remaining distance between us and one of my oldest friends. His extended hand connected with mine as I pulled him in for a big hug. Damn, we hadn't seen each other in years. How the time flies when life is all too consuming, especially those past few months.

"Kael Stonebridge! What the hell are you doing here?" I asked as we finally broke apart and took a step back from each other.

"Adara and I moved back from California two weeks ago. I meant to look you up but have been so busy with the move and everything. I'm so happy I ran in to you. It's been, what, like five years since we saw each other, right? We have a lot to catch up on, man."

"You're damn right we do." We both stood there watching one another, the surprise of having him standing in front of me still not completely registering. I was so lost in memories of us growing up, including all the trouble we used to get into, I'd completely forgotten about Sara.

She reached out and gripped my hand, the warmth of her palm speeding up the beat of my heart. One touch was all it took. One small point of contact and I forgot all about my long-lost buddy.

As soon as all of my attention flitted to the woman on my right, Kael intently took notice. He, like many others, was simply not used to seeing me with any female. Unless, of course, it was our old college days and women were nothing but a distraction.

Feeling as if I was betraying Sara on some level by even recalling such memories, I returned all my attention to the present. Even though I knew my good friend was married to an amazing woman, and even though I knew he would never over-step his bounds, I leaned close to Sara and gave her a kiss. It was an innate reaction to claim her in front of him. In reality, he was another male who had to be made aware of the simple truth that Sara was all mine.

My actions weren't obvious, but Kael knew exactly what I was doing. When I glanced back over at him, I saw him smirk, his attentions roving between the both of us.

Releasing her hand, I gripped her waist and pulled her into me. "Please forgive my rudeness, honey. This is one of my oldest friends in the world, Kael Stonebridge. Kael, this is my Sara." They quickly shook hands. The sight of Sara touching another man did crazy things to me. Normally, I would have been upset, causing some sort of scene. Her touches were only for me. But I reeled it in, knowing full well she was merely being polite. Kael saw it, though. He took notice of the fleeting tick in my jaw, the quick flare of my nostrils.

"*Your* Sara? Wow, who *is* this guy in front of me?" He chuckled. "You never referred to anyone as yours before. You must be pretty damn special to my friend here," he claimed, turning his attentions back on Sara.

"You better believe she is. I was merely drifting through life before she came into my world." A blush stole across her cheeks as I spoke, the sight instantly exciting me. I didn't know what it was about the heat of her skin, but it always did strange things to me.

I'd been so consumed with Kael and Sara, I hadn't taken notice as to where his wife was. Glancing around behind him, I asked, "Where's Adara?"

"She's in one of those shops several doors down. Speaking of, I should probably go and get her; otherwise, we'll be here all day." I laughed. I'd known Adara a long time, and shopping was one of her most favorite indulgences. "Hey, you two have to come over for dinner this week. We're almost done unpacking, so it's perfect timing."

"Of course. We'd love to come. Are you still at the same number?" I asked. We'd kept in contact with each other over the years, but I knew he had some issues with a client of his a while back so he had to change his cell number. I was simply making sure he hadn't changed it since.

"You know it. Great. Listen, I have to run now, but call me later and we'll set everything up. Sara, it was a true pleasure to meet you," he declared before taking hold of her hand. Before I could react, he pulled her close and kissed her cheek.

He's pushing it.

"All right there, Casanova. Enough. Remember, you're married, plus this woman here is off-limits," I reminded him.

The fucker knew he was riling me up, but he didn't care. "I would never think of it." If Kael wasn't my good friend, he would've been on his ass right then, staring up at me in disbelief. But he was and I knew he wasn't hitting on Sara, so I allowed him to remain upright.

"Give Adara my best," I called out as he turned and walked away.

"He seemed nice," she said, watching him disappear into a store twenty feet away.

"He is. He's truly one of the greatest guys I've ever met."

"I'm assuming you guys go way back."

"Yeah, we grew up together. We were thick as thieves until we were in our mid twenties. We even went in on numerous projects. But then his work took him to California, where he's been all this time."

"Well, I'm excited to go to dinner and get to know him and his wife. It should be fun." A genuine smile tickled her lips as she spoke.

"You'll love them," I promised as we made our way inside one of the many shops on the street.

~19~

Sara

Three days later, Alek informed me we were going to have dinner at Kael and Adara's house. I was really looking forward to getting to know them better. I'd only briefly met Kael, but he seemed like a genuine person. Any man who put my guy in such a good mood was definitely worth spending more time with.

Thankfully, my interaction with him was brief because when I'd first laid eyes on him, I almost bugged out. He was no comparison to Alek—no one was, in my opinion—but the man was hot. His penetrating blue eyes drew me right in, almost as if he was peering into the deepest parts of my psyche. I wasn't interested in him, furthest thing from reality. But I knew a fine specimen of a male when I feasted my eyes on one.

Having no doubt I'd hit it off with Alek's friends, I became excited at the prospect of having another couple to hang around with from time to time. In no way was I complaining about spending time alone with Alek, but someone new to give me a better insight to my guy was always welcome. Never mind, I was beyond curious to see him interact with someone who wasn't an employee.

We arrived at their house around seven o'clock. They told us we would be having a late dinner but wanted us to arrive early enough to have a tour of their new home.

Kael greeted us at the door and surprisingly welcomed me with a big, warm hug. I wasn't sure, but I could've sworn I heard Alek growl behind me.

As soon as I stepped foot inside their foyer, I was overwhelmed with a sense of home, which probably had a lot to do with the fact there was a woman's touch involved. Alek's house was wonderful, but I could definitely tell from the décor, while appealing, that a man lived there. Alone.

We were led toward the kitchen where the woman of the house was checking on dinner. Whatever she was making smelled wonderful. I hadn't even realized how hungry I was until the wafting aroma filled my nose.

As soon as Adara saw us, she put her towel on the counter and rushed right over. First she approached Alek, kissing him on the cheek before enveloping him in a big hug. Then she turned her sights on me. "Sara, it's such a pleasure to meet you." She took me in her arms, and I couldn't help but be affected by her warm welcome. She seemed so genuine and down-to-earth, someone I knew I would get along great with right away.

She instantly intrigued me. Never mind the fact she was gorgeous. She reminded me of a Victoria's Secret model with her lithe body, long blonde hair and stunning features. All she was missing were the runway angel wings.

"It's great to meet you, as well, Adara. Alek has told me such nice things about you." I turned toward Kael. "About both of you. Thank you so much for inviting me tonight."

While I was chatting with Adara, Alek brushed past me and moved closer to the stove. Leaning over, he did his best to inspect our future meal. "Adara, I didn't know you knew how to cook." His brow cocked in amusement.

"Of course I do. Who do you think has been feeding your friend all these years?"

"It's true, man. She keeps me fed. And fed well," he joked as he patted his trim stomach.

After some quick chit-chat, they indulged us with a tour of their place. It was smaller than Alek's, but the richness in character definitely made up for whatever they lacked in size.

The original woodwork was displayed throughout the home. Every fine detail and etching caught the eye as you walked from room to room. Beautiful artwork adorned the walls, enticing me to stop and stare for moments at a time.

Half an hour into our tour, Adara announced dinner would be ready in another twenty minutes. "Why don't you guys go in the den and have a quick drink," she encouraged as she lightly pushed both men toward the other room. She took hold of my arm and led me back toward the kitchen. "We'll call you when it's ready."

Kael slapped his friend on the back, obviously reveling in the fact they were allowed some long-awaited guy-bonding minutes. "Sounds good to us, babe. Let us know if you need our assistance," he shouted as they hurriedly walked away.

Alek looked back to catch me before I disappeared around the corner. "I won't be long, babe." He sounded as if our separation was causing him some sort of discomfort.

"Come on, lover boy. She'll be fine without you hovering over her for a few minutes." His friend drew him away before he could protest.

"Can I help?" I asked as we headed back into the kitchen.

"Sure. You can grab what we need for the salad." She pointed to the refrigerator. "Everything should be on the second shelf." While I busied myself with my new job assignment, Adara put the finishing touches on the casserole. As soon as the smell hit me, my stomach growled. It was then I realized it'd been hours since I'd last had anything to eat.

During mid-chop of the mushrooms, curiosity about my host suddenly became too much. I decided to dig a little. "Adara. Such a beautiful but unusual name. I've never heard anything like it before."

"Thank you. Yes, it is unusual. It's an old Irish name which means fire. Ask my husband and he'll tell you I surely live up to the name."

She laughed and removed the dish from the oven before turning around to face me. "So, tell me, Sara, how long have you and Alek known each other?"

"Not long. Although, it feels like I've known him forever." My mind drifted off to thoughts of my glorious man, even though we'd only parted ways fifteen minutes before. I had it bad and I knew it. I tried to play it cool, but I was sure I failed miserably.

"Well, when you're meant to be together, it seems like you can't imagine a time when they weren't part of your life. Trust me, I speak from experience."

"I know what you mean," I replied, her comment surprisingly insightful.

Giving her masterpiece one more look, she announced, "Well, it's time we call the men to the table."

~~~~

After a scrumptious dinner, we relaxed with coffee and homemade apple pie.

Kael was the first to start revealing secrets of his dear friend. "Sara, I must say, I was pleasantly surprised when I ran in to the two of you the other day and saw how taken he was with you. But it's a good thing. A great thing, in fact."

Alek leaned over and kissed my temple, showing me he agreed with Kael's sentiments.

"It sure is," Adara chimed in. "It's about time he settled down, and he couldn't have picked a better woman." They were both so sweet, but all of the *settling down* talk was making me a bit uneasy, mainly because our relationship was still a little fragile. Every day, we were making progress, but I was fearful the smallest thing could upset the balance we'd been able to build and maintain.

Trying to switch the subject, I turned the spotlight onto them. "How did you guys meet?" I asked, finishing off the rest of my delicious pie.

They lovingly glanced at each other before speaking. It was really quite sweet. Kael spoke first. "Do you want to tell the story, or should I?"

"I'll tell it since you like to omit certain details every time you spew your side of it." Adara smiled at her husband as he clasped her hand in his.

"How could I forget any detail about you, sweetheart?"

"All right, all right. Just tell us the story and stop being so mushy, you two." Alek feigned annoyance, rolling his eyes and shaking his head. But I knew those two people meant the world to him. I saw it in the way he glanced at them, the deep connection they all shared evident in his eyes. And in his bright smile.

Taking the lead, Adara kissed her husband before she started speaking. "Well, I have to mention that the first time I laid eyes on Kael, I was immediately smitten. I only had the physical to go on, and he *is* gorgeous." She leaned over and gave him another kiss before continuing. Something in her smirk told me the next part of her story was going to be good. "But if I'm being completely honest, I couldn't stand him the first time I met him."

"Hey!" Kael retorted, a faux-hurt look splayed all over his face. I was sure he knew exactly where the story was headed, no doubt their tale being re-told to many people. Her declaration definitely intrigued me. Their love for one another was evident, so I was curious to find out how they worked through whatever issues they had during the beginning of their relationship.

"Oh, calm down. I love you now more than ever." She rubbed his arm, trying to soothe his fake wounded ego. "Anyway, as I was saying, I couldn't stand him when I first met him. He was so cocky and unbelievably forward. While my body reacted to the mere sight of him, my head tried to warn me he was nothing but trouble."

"If it's any consolation, Adara, I didn't care for the guy either when I first met him," Alek teased.

Kael instantly laughed and leaned forward on the table. "Real nice, man. We were only in kindergarten, and you know you stole my blocks."

"I don't know what you're talking about," Alek retorted.

"Uh-huh. Whatever you have to tell yourself." Kael latched on to his wife's hand again, unable to allow any time to go by without touching her. It was sweet.

Several seconds of silence passed, but it was in those quick moments I witnessed a level to their love I'd not seen before. Granted, I'd only just met them, but the way Kael watched his wife was mesmerizing. He adored her. He seemed enthralled with her every word. The way he watched her movements was as if he was constantly bombarded with sinful thoughts of her. His enrapture with her was enough to make me squirm in my own damn seat.

When I glanced in her direction, the love she held for him danced freely in her eyes. Her world started and ended with the man sitting next to her. I could tell she was a strong-willed woman, but when it came to her husband, she would risk it all for their love. I just knew it. Being in their company was a gift. It was hard to explain exactly, but I knew I was in the presence of true love.

But oftentimes, such an intense love surely came with intense passion of all kinds, including arguments. And if anyone understood that, it was me.

Kael whispered something into Adara's ear, and it was enough to make her blush. She lightly coughed to regain her composure before continuing with her story. "I was at a nightclub with a group of my friends for a girls' night. I didn't want to go out that evening because I was still upset over a recent breakup, but they threatened to drag me out in my pajamas if I didn't get dressed." Her eyes were fixated on me, as if I was the only one she was speaking to.

"That guy was a loser. I don't even know why you went out with him in the first place," Kael grumbled. Years later, I could see the situation still plagued him. Was it the fact there was mention of another man, or the fact his wife had been upset at all?

"I know, sweetheart. I was simply biding my time until you came along." She stroked his cheek, doing her best to comfort him.

"Anyway, we were all having a good time, drinking and dancing, when all of a sudden I caught a glimpse of this man," she said as she thumbed over toward Kael. "I almost stumbled over my own feet I was so taken with the sight of him. Unfortunately, so were all the other women there that night. In fact, he walked in with two bimbos on his arm." There was a slight jealous tone to her words, even after all those years.

Unfortunately, I could totally relate. I hated to think about the women who came before me. I didn't want to share Alek at any time, period.

"I watched him for a while, being careful not to make eye contact for fear I would appear as wanton as every other female there. What I could see was him flirting with not only the women he walked in with, but also every female he came into contact with. I thought he was a player, for sure, and in an effort to protect my heart, I stayed as far away from him as possible. I allowed myself to admire him from a distance, but it was as far as I was willing to let it go."

"Ah, but you couldn't resist me for long, my sweet," Kael teased as he swung his arm around her shoulder.

"I resisted you far longer than anyone ever did."

"That you did." He sighed. "That you did."

As she continued her story, her demeanor slightly shifted. It was subtle, but I picked up on it. It was almost as if she was re-living the entire encounter all over again.

"At one point in the evening, I was waiting at the bar for drinks when he came out of nowhere and pushed up next to me, asking me if I wanted to leave with him, go somewhere more private."

I couldn't help myself. "What did you say?" I blurted out. All eyes were on me, my fascination with their story amusing to everyone there.

"I looked him straight in the eye and told him 'Not in a million years, pal.' Yeah, I called him 'pal.' Needless to say, I piqued his interest. Can you imagine? Some woman *not* tripping over herself to leave with this fine specimen?" Her sarcasm drove home her point.

Kael's mouth gaped open as he slightly shook his head. "I know *I* couldn't believe it. I knew right away this woman was different from all the others. Honestly, I wasn't used to anyone telling me 'no,' so when I ran across this one,"—he bumped Adara's shoulder lightly with his own—"I was thoroughly intrigued."

"He followed me around for the rest of the evening, continuing to ask for my number, pestering me to go out with him. I answered with a resounding *no* to each and every one of his advances. I knew I was getting under his skin as the night wore on, but I thought it only fair since he had mine burning up. I came to find out later on one of my girlfriends gave him my phone number on the side. I could have killed her at first, but have grown to be so grateful over time. She was even my maid of honor at our wedding."

"So, did he call you constantly? How long after you first met did you decide to go out with him and give him a chance?" I was so enthralled with their story; I had to know more.

"Two months." She smirked.

"Yeah, two damn months!" Kael interjected. "Can you believe that shit?" He grabbed her and quickly pulled her onto his lap, lavishing her with a passionate kiss. "But she was well worth the wait."

"Yes, I was," Adara confirmed with a quick nod of her beautiful head.

"So, we began dating, cautiously on my part in the beginning, even though I was already in love with him the first week into our relationship. I know it was quick, but I just knew, you know?" She was looking at me when she asked her question. I nodded and smiled.

"And it's been a dream ever since." The look Adara gave him was amusing. Kael knit his brow in quick confusion.

"Uh, no, it wasn't. Not for a while. You were always questioning everything I did. But I never let you get away with it, not once, which is probably why we argued like we did. Come to think of it, you still do have your challenging ways about you. But I've learned when to pick my battles. It's simply easier on everyone." They were lost in each other, a silent message passing between them before they turned their eyes back onto their guests.

"Sounds familiar," I blurted before I could stop my mouth from moving. Alek turned to face me, wondering where the hell that came from. I bit my lower lip and laughed, seeing as I didn't know what else to do.

"Do tell, Sara," Adara prompted.

"Yeah, do tell," Alek chimed in. His smile gave me comfort, allowing me the freedom to speak my mind freely.

"Well, what I meant was Alek does the same thing to me, challenging my independence."

I was going to explain further, but of course he had to put his two cents in and explain. "No, I don't challenge your independence. I encourage it, just not when your safety is involved, which happens to be a lot of the time."

Refusing to indulge his crazy, redundant statement, I chose to focus all of my attention back on Adara. "Yeah, well, I haven't learned to pick my battles yet, Adara. Hopefully, soon."

"Hopefully," Alek added.

I shook my head and smirked. I was relieved I could talk freely with his friends. Luckily, Adara and I were forming a bond. We could relate to each other in the sense we both had men in our lives we couldn't imagine being without, but who tested us every step of the way.

We said our goodbyes a little while later, thanking them again for such a wonderful evening. Before Alek opened the car door for me, he turned me around and crushed me to his massive frame. He looked into my eyes for some of the longest seconds before descending to claim me. He asked for permission to enter my mouth with the tantalizing flick of his warm tongue on my lower lip, and I was only too happy to oblige. But our entanglement ended as quickly as it started when Kael yelled from the front entrance of his home for us to get a room.

We both laughed and took it as our cue to continue in private.

~20~

Alek

We went back to my place afterwards, talking about what a good time we had with my dear friends. It was the perfect ending to the enjoyable evening.

Settling in for the night, we snuggled close on the couch, the flames from the roaring fire dancing in front of us. Entertaining us.

To say I was living the dream would be an understatement. I'd finally met the woman I was destined for. Even though we'd had some hurdles to overcome, I wouldn't change a damn thing. Sara meant the world to me, and I would do everything in my power to make sure she was happy. Not only with us but with life in general. It was my job to ensure not only her safety but her pleasure, as well.

It was my own personal mission to make sure my woman was satisfied, in all aspects of life.

I cradled her body from behind, the curve of her ass already exciting me. My cock thickened the more she wriggled around, trying to get a little more comfortable. I knew she felt me because she pushed herself against me. Groaning into her ear, my breath cascaded over her flushed skin. She squirmed a little more and as I put my hand on her waist to pull her hard against me, she chose a topic which killed the mood immediately.

"Alek, what happened to your sister?" She held her breath in anticipation of my answer. She didn't think I noticed, but I did. Her body tensed as soon as the last word left her lips.

Why now?

I didn't respond at first, still dueling with myself as to what I should or even *wanted* to say. I couldn't ignore her questions forever, but was I ready to delve into it right then?

Finally, I decided to give her something.

"She died." Knowing my response was obvious, I waited for her to press me further.

"I know. You mentioned it once." Sara took a deep breath before asking, "How did she die?"

More silence.

If I was going to finally have this conversation with her, I had to prepare myself. I leaned in and kissed the crown of her head before rising from the couch.

I needed a damn drink.

Slowly walking toward the corner of the room, I poured myself a stiff one. The dark liquid goaded me, threatening to tell all my secrets if I consumed too much. Putting the top back on the decanter, I walked away with only a small amount of liquor in my glass, knowing too well I'd fall prey to the seduction of too much alcohol if I didn't control myself. Normally, I didn't have a problem. But talking about my sister, although a rare occasion, always put me overboard. I drank to excess if I lived in the past.

I had to be careful.

Thankfully, Sara was looking on with genuine concern for me.

She would give me the strength I needed to push through it.

Her and a small amount of scotch.

I loved my sister, even in death. Nothing would ever break our bond. Doing my best to remain strong, I fought back the emotion trying to tear forth from me. Aware my eyes had become glassy in my despair, I turned away from her. I didn't want her to see me that way. I didn't want her to witness me break.

Swallowing another mouthful of the amber liquid, I deemed it time to tell my story.

My sister's dreadful, tragic story.

Once I was seated next to Sara on the couch, I began. She rested her hand on my knee for comfort. It helped.

"Mia was such a wonderful person, so full of life. I still can't believe she's gone." I took a much needed breath. "The world truly lost a great soul when she was taken from us."

I glanced down at my trembling hands as I spoke my next words.

"She was only twenty years old when she was murdered."

~21~

Sara

Oh, my God! I'd assumed she was sick or died from the result of an accident. I would've never guessed someone had killed her, taken her life on purpose.

I didn't say a word, knowing he needed to tell her story in his own time. Rubbing his leg, I tried my best to offer him my support and strength. I knew he hadn't talked about his sister in a long time, and I wanted him to know I was there for him. I would do my best to console him if he broke down.

Just when I thought he might have shut down, words tumbled from his beautiful lips. "Mia was two years my junior. She idolized me growing up, but I never took advantage of it. I always looked out for her, no matter what. It was my job as her big brother. Other than normal sibling squabbles, we got along great. My incessant need to keep her safe," he said, glancing over at me, "drove her mad sometimes." A small smile tipped his lips as he saw the irony in his statement. "Her biggest complaint was when I refused to allow her to attend any parties I was invited to. They were simply no place for young girls. I was doing my best to keep her innocent for as long as possible. Since I was the man of the house, I took on the role of her protector, and I played the part to the best of my ability."

My heart bled for him. I couldn't even imagine being responsible for another human being, to try and protect them from harm only to have them ripped away from me. I'd lost people during my short life, but it was different. Alek was a man who was stoically strong, always in control, domineering and powerful. But right then, he seemed to be simply a man writhing around in a world of pain. Lost and alone.

It affected me deeply.

It tore at the core of my being.

"It's okay," I said, continuing to rub his leg.

He smiled, but it never reached his eyes. "One night, Mia was at a party I attended. When I confronted her and told her to go home, she yelled at me, reminding me I wasn't her father and since she was eighteen, she could do whatever she wanted. And I knew, knew I couldn't control her actions forever, but I sure as hell would try to, for as long as I could. My only concern was for her safety and well-being."

Boy, do those words sound familiar.

He reached out and clutched my hand, searching for the strength to go on. He found it when I tangled my fingers with his and gave him a little squeeze.

"It was at that party she met Michael Covington." He physically cringed at the sound of the guy's name. "I should have pressed harder for her to leave. I should have dragged her out of there kicking and screaming. I'll forever carry around the guilt of not doing more. I can't rid myself of the feeling that if I had forced her to leave with me, she would still be alive today." He shook his head. "Anyway, as soon as I saw the look in her eyes when she caught his attention, well...it was all downhill from there."

"Why? Did you know this Michael?" I tried not to ask too many questions, but I had to know.

"I knew *of* him. He wasn't in my circle of friends, but he was a friend of a friend of a friend." He waved his hand about. "You know how that goes." I nodded. "I knew enough about him to know he was bad news. Let's just say he wasn't too nice to his girlfriends." When I furrowed my brow, not quite understanding, he clarified his statement. "I'd heard from numerous sources he had quite the temper, and more than one girlfriend had received the brunt of his anger. I even witnessed it for myself on one occasion. I rushed in to try to break it up, and we ended up fighting each other. Friends of mine broke up the fight, but not before I got in one last punch. And the girl he was pounding on had the nerve to be mad at *me*!"

"You guys were young. Sometimes, young women don't understand they shouldn't tolerate such behavior. It's really sad."

"Yeah, I suppose," he reflected. "I knew what type of person Michael was, and as soon as I saw them flirting with each other, I stepped in and tried to put a stop to it. Mia and I got into a big fight, and she took off. I found out later on Michael had found her and given her a ride home.

"Soon after, they started dating and at first, she seemed really happy. But I knew eventually he was going to hurt her. He was a bad guy, and there was no way he was going to change simply because he was dating my little sister. I warned him on several occasions that if he ever laid a finger on her, I would kill him. He would laugh and tell me he loved her and nothing I could do or say would ever break them up. He reminded me she loved him and would never listen to me." He looked away for a minute, his recollections obviously dragging him under. "And the sad thing was...he was right. She was so blind to his evil ways, even when I tried to tell her about his past girlfriends. She was naïve, never believing he would ever do those things to her."

He stopped talking suddenly, released my hand, stood and moved toward the window. Glancing outside, he appeared as if he was summoning the strength to continue. "It was three months into their relationship when I first noticed the marks. Mia was coming out of the bathroom one day and I saw a nasty welt across her back, slightly above where her towel was covering her. Right near her shoulder blades. When I confronted her about it, she said it was nothing. She tried to play it off as if she fell or knocked into something. You know, typical responses from someone being abused. I told her flat-out I didn't believe her, that I knew Michael was hitting her. She denied it, of course, saying he loved her and wouldn't do such a thing. Knowing

I would go after him, she never told me the truth. But what she didn't know was I didn't need her confirmation.

"The more I pushed her to leave him, the more she withdrew from me, an action which hurt me the most. I was only trying to protect her, but she didn't want to have anything to do with me." I knew he was breaking. He was still facing away from me, his shoulders slumped in defeat.

"Oh, Alek, she was young," I offered. "She was in love with him, or at least she thought it was love. He was manipulating her, probably blaming her for making him hurt her. She was probably so embarrassed she allowed him to treat her like that she shied away from you." My heart picked up speed, angry toward a situation from so long before. I wished I could have been there for him then. Little did I know at the time I had my own tragedy waiting for me not far into the future.

"It still hurt me deeply just the same. Mia became pregnant after about a year. He asked her to marry him, and she was happy to agree. I begged her not to do it. I pleaded with her to leave him, to come home and raise her baby with us. I warned her if she stayed with Michael, he would eventually kill her. She thought I was being crazy, but I could see by the look in her eye she believed me, even if she didn't want to admit it out loud."

Alek walked back toward the couch and took a seat next to me, reaching for my hand once again. "They were married by a justice of the peace three months later, and she moved in with him. Away from me. I tried to call her numerous times a week, but he would always answer her phone, telling me she wasn't available to talk. He was alienating her from her family and friends, making sure he was the only one in her life. I even went over there a few times, banging on the door and threatening him, but it didn't do any good. Every call I placed to the cops was a wasted effort. They told me unless she pressed charges, there was nothing they could do. I felt so helpless."

My heart broke for Alek. Such a heavy burden he carried around with him. I wished there was something I could have done to take away his pain, but there wasn't. He had to live with the loss of his sister for the rest of his life. I only hoped he wouldn't carry around such guilt. He was barely an adult, for God's sake, all of twenty-two years old when she died.

He continued on with the rest of the story, speaking quicker than before to try to end the pain sooner. "It was late one night when I received the dreaded visit from the cops. They told me my baby sister was dead." Alek took a quick breather, hesitating to finish his story. It was almost as if revealing the final part of the story made it real. All over again.

"The bastard slit her throat, killing her and my unborn nephew. It wasn't bad enough he beat her repeatedly. He had to go ahead and end her life and do so in such a horrific way."

My breath caught in my throat. Instant sadness and fury raced through me, gripping my insides in a vise so tight I had trouble breathing. "Oh, my God. Oh, my God," I kept repeating. "Alek. I am so sorry." I didn't know what else to do but throw my arms around his neck and sob for him, for the burden he'd carried around since that tragic day. For the loss of his sister and her unborn child.

For the loss of a love that would never flourish to anything beyond a naïve young woman and her older brother who was forever trying to protect her.

"What happened to him? To Michael? Is he in jail? Please, tell me he'll never see the light of day again."

"No, he's dead." He said the words with such finality it actually sent shivers up my spine.

"How did he die?" I cautiously asked, preparing myself for his answer.

"I didn't kill him, if that's what you're thinking, Sara. Although, I wish I had been the lucky one to take him out of this world. No, while he was out on bail, awaiting the trial, he was drunk and mouthed off to the wrong person. He was shot dead in a seedy bar. He died like the animal he was, with a bullet to the head. It's the only thing which brings me some sort of comfort, knowing he isn't breathing the same air I am."

Even though I knew it was extremely hard for Alek to talk about his sister, he almost seemed relieved to have been able to share it with me. I didn't really know what to say, except, "Thank you for telling me about Mia. I know it was hard for you to do."

He pulled me close and tipped my chin upward so he could gaze into my eyes. "I think my overwhelming need to protect you is driven by the fact I couldn't save my sister. What I mean to say is, I would have this fierce need to keep you safe regardless, but my sister's death fuels it even more. I don't know what I would do if something ever happened to you. It would be like the last good part of me was stolen. I wouldn't be able to go on." He squeezed my hands in his. "So please try not to be too upset with me when I'm making my demands. They're irrational to you, but they make perfect sense to me. Your safety is my sanity."

"I do understand your need to protect me a little more now, Alek, but it doesn't mean all of a sudden I'm going to give in to all of your overbearing tendencies." Before he could interrupt with his rebuttal, I cut him off. "I'll try to be more understanding and more accommodating, but it's hard for me to give up any part of my independence. This will be a work in progress. I'm just warning you now."

"I know. I wouldn't expect anything less from you, sweetheart. Your strong will is one of the things I love most about you, although it drives me insane most of the time. But thank you for at least giving me what I want."

"Wait...I didn't say *that*. Let's not get ahead of ourselves here."

He laughed. He was teasing me. "You can't blame a guy for trying." I was so elated to see my man smile, even if it was for a brief moment.

Hopefully, he'd be able to release some of the guilt he'd been carrying around for the greater part of a decade.

~22~

Alek

Climbing the stairs, I did nothing but reflect on the evening. We'd spent a wonderful time with two people who were very special to me. I loved that Sara got along with them so well, and they with her. Envisioning a night out in the near future with everyone managed to put a small smile on my face.

Soon, thoughts of my sister filled my head again. Mia. I missed her so much, time doing nothing to heal the hole in my heart. Normally, I would have shut down each and every time anyone asked about her, but I knew I had to tell Sara the story sooner or later. Since she pushed the issue, I figured there was no better time than the present.

It was painful. I'm not going to lie, but I'm happy I did it. The guilt still ate at me, but my heart was a little lighter. All thanks to the beautiful woman walking in front of me.

I knew the story I threw at her feet affected her. I made her cry, for Christ's sake, a reaction I never expected. Or did I? I knew Sara had a big heart, so why was it a shock she wept for me? In truth, I wasn't used to really opening up to anyone. She was the first woman I'd ever let inside and to be quite honest, while I reveled in it, it freaked me out a little.

Sara made me feel vulnerable.

She didn't know it, but it was the truth.

Trying my hardest to not succumb to my own desires, wanting to give myself the evening to recuperate emotionally, I looked down at my feet with each step I took. Her phenomenal ass was beckoning to me, though, and I wasn't sure how much longer I was going to be able to hold out. With every sway of her hips and every bounce of her tits, I weakened more and more.

Confliction took hold and shook me like a rag doll. The closer we came to my bedroom, the more my thoughts were overrun with images of her writhing underneath me in ecstasy.

"Are you all right, Alek?" she asked, turning to press her hand on my chest, right over my heart.

"Yes," I answered. "I think I am." Hating the distance between us, I grabbed her hips and pulled her close. One kiss was all it took to unleash the beast inside.

The weight of my guilt was suspended for a time, and I was going to take full advantage.

"I'm going to take a quick shower and when I'm done, I want you naked on my bed. Waiting for me." I knew my demand was coming out of left field, but she did it to me every time. I slapped her on the ass as I headed toward the bathroom.

"But...uh...are you sure? I mean, are you up for it?" She was genuinely concerned for my emotional state, and it was touching. What she didn't realize was I needed the distraction. Badly.

I knew everything would be all right if I could just lose myself in her.

In us.

Knowing I wouldn't be able to explain it to her the right way, I simply nodded before I turned and walked away.

~23~

Sara

He didn't even give me a chance to respond before the door closed behind him, the spray of the shower the very next sound I heard.

I tried to put myself in Alek's shoes. If I'd shared a story like the one he told me, how would I feel? Would I want to go to bed with those thoughts running through my head, over and over? Or would I want him to take me, to make me forget, even if for a short while?

For me, it was a no-brainer.

I would choose to forget.

As instructed, I undressed and laid on the bed, ready and waiting for him to make me scream his name. While the wait was driving me insane, the anticipation built the more he left me alone with my own thoughts.

An indescribable ache bloomed between my legs. *If he doesn't open that damn door in the next thirty seconds, I'm going to go crazy.*

"What are you thinking about, baby?" He startled me as his voice boomed around the room while strolling toward the bed, a predatory gait to his walk. He looked positively delicious, covered in nothing but a white towel slung low on his hips. Mesmerized by the sheer sight of him, I almost combusted when he untucked the edge of the soft fabric and tousled it through his dark, wet hair.

Leaving him completely exposed.

I'd feasted my eyes on him more times than I could count, always a needy mess, and this time was no different. My eyes widened, a throaty sound escaping my lips as I blatantly checked him out from head to toe.

Taking two steps in my direction, he tossed the towel aside and gripped his thick cock, licking his lips as he stroked himself from the tip all the way down. Then back up again.

He arched a brow. "What's the matter, sweetheart? You seem a little flushed."

I heard him speak, but the words sounded all jumbled. The only thing I could focus on was the way he teased himself. His fingers clenched his arousal, and as he was about to torture me again, I rose on my knees and placed my hands on my thighs. I leaned forward so I could see him better.

"Can I help you with something?" He knew exactly what he was doing to me, and he was loving it.

But so was I.

"Do it again," I begged, my fingertips digging into the sensitive skin of my legs.

"Hmmmm...like this?" He took another step in my direction, his fingers never leaving the soft steel of his erection. Locking eyes with me, he teased his sensitive flesh with one more small stroke.

Then stopped.

Altogether.

Before I could utter a complaint, he turned on his heel and moved toward the chair nestled near the window. I was mesmerized with every corded muscle of his back as he moved, every twitch of his excited skin as he walked away from me. His delicious ass was a thing of beauty. *There should be songs written about it.*

Lost in a haze of my own horniness, I hadn't noticed he sat in the chair, legs spread and ready for something. But what? What was he doing all the way over there when I was clearly ready to go for some much needed lovin'?

"Why are you so far away?"

"This distance is perfect," he answered quickly, his hands resting on his stomach, hiding most of his cock from my view. To say I was disappointed was an understatement.

I was so confused. *Can't he see I'm a mess?* Crawling toward the edge of the bed, I made a move to get down, but the deep timber of his voice stopped me immediately.

"No."

One word and I halted instantly. The look in his eyes told me he was just as excited, but his refusal to ravage me was slowly killing me.

The more his gaze drifted over my naked body, the more self-conscious I became. *What is he doing?*

Moving back on the bed, I grabbed the blanket and quickly tried to cover myself, the sly smirk on his face prompting me to move faster.

"What are you doing, Sara? I told you I wanted you naked on my bed. Not naked underneath my covers." He leaned forward in the chair. "Try to cover up again, and I'll redden your ass. Unless of course, you *want* me to do that."

He flustered me. He rendered me to nothing more than a babbling idiot. "Yes...I mean no...I mean...I...I don't know what to say," I proclaimed as I tossed the corner of the covers aside.

Totally dismissing my little stammering episode, he relaxed against the back of the chair. Sexually charged minutes passed in silence before he finally spoke. "Lie back on the bed. Good. Now spread your legs. Wider. Put your finger in your mouth. Sara? Do it," he demanded.

Where is this all coming from?

He isn't going to ask me to...

~24~

Alek

"I want you to pleasure yourself. I want you to play with your clit and make yourself nice and wet."

My cock twitched in the heat of my palm. The sight of Sara spread wide in front of me, her pussy glistening in anticipation of what I was going to demand next was pure torture.

No way in hell was I going to stop, though.

"I...I can't," she whispered, reservation strangling the life from her words. If I hadn't needed such a distraction, I wouldn't have pushed her, instead choosing another night to slowly bring her around to the thought of masturbating in front of me.

Sara was ballsy, more so with me than anyone else in her life, but she was still shy, continuing to blush from time to time when mere words were spoken. I'd tell her what I wished to do to her and all of a sudden, a beautiful redness would pierce her skin, the color so alluring I purposely dirtied up my sex talk even more.

"You can. Just close your eyes and pretend your hand is mine, caressing your sweet skin, dipping inside you to feel your warmth." She remained still until I pleaded, the need in my voice telling of many things. I wanted our experience to continue, to make me so damn hot I'd have to hold myself back from pouncing on her, driving into her until she found Heaven. But I also needed to know she was willing to help me; the emotional numbness I was searching for was all in her control.

I needed her to release me...in every way possible.

"Please, sweetheart."

The understanding in her eyes was enough to push her past the brink of shyness, her hands pinching and teasing her nipples until they pebbled.

Her mouth parted. She licked her lips. A small moan escaped, and I thought I was going to have a mess in my hands.

"That's it. Now, show me how you make yourself come."

While one hand continued to tease her nipple, her other cascaded over her beautiful skin, slowly moving toward her pussy. The wait was agony. Her fingers drew circles against the flat of her belly, teasing me unmercifully. She stayed there for what seemed like forever. Finally, she dipped lower, brushing over the small strip of hair she kept neatly trimmed.

Then she made contact.

As soon as her finger found her clit, her back arched off the bed and her legs spread wider. An intoxicating gasp broke free as she dipped further still and pushed a finger inside her tight heat.

"How does that feel?" I asked, tightening my grip. I was doing my best to hold off, but the more she squirmed under her own touch, the more tempting it was to let go and stroke my cock until I found my release.

"So good," she purred. Even the lilt of her voice pushed me to the brink. "Hmmmmm...so good," she repeated.

I could only go so far before I lost all control and claimed her. I was surely testing my resolve. Never had I initiated such a scene from anyone else before.

Everything was different with Sara.

I wanted to own her.

I wanted her to own me.

"Push another finger inside. That's it. Do you love the fullness? Are you picturing they're my fingers pleasuring you? Tell me," I demanded. "Tell me how much you love fucking yourself. For me."

Goddamn it! I was going to come any second if I didn't get a grip. *No pun intended.*

No, I only wanted to come deep inside her. I wasn't going to waste my orgasm on my own fucking hand.

"I love it," she moaned. Her breaths were short and choppy. While I wanted to hear her scream out her release, she wasn't going to come from her own touch. Instead, she was going to convulse all over me while I thrust deep inside her, over and over again.

"Don't come yet. Bring yourself right to the edge, but don't let go. Not until I tell you."

I could tell she was close, her moans coming hard and fast.

"Sara..." I warned.

"Alek...please. Please...I need you. Right now!" Her hips bucked against her hand, searching for the end of her pleasure. "I'm gonna come, Alek, please..." she begged.

"Fuck!" I yelled before clearing the distance between us. I quickly sheathed myself with a condom before pushing her hand away, the absence of her fingers almost too much for her to bear. A few more seconds and she would have tipped over, falling fast into her bed of bliss.

With one thrust, I pushed deep inside, her tight, warm walls gripping every thick inch of me. Her back arched off the bed completely, her nails raking over the bristling skin of my back.

We didn't last long.

Moments later I swallowed her screams with my mouth, the heat of her tongue pushing me to release myself right along with her.

~25~

Sara

"You got it. We'll see you then." Alek ended his conversation as he walked through the front door of the shop, finding my undivided attention was solely on him. Watching him. Studying him.

I would never tire of the man, my blatant perusal of him telling the tale.

"Hi."

"Hello, beautiful." His sexy smile made me sigh. Loudly. Two words and a wink and I was a puddle of mush already.

Standing nearby, there were two women milling around. Or at least they were before Alek walked in. Clearly, they were watching him. *My* man. One of them whispered something in the other's ear then smirked. I didn't like it. Not one bit. Subtlety definitely wasn't their strong suit.

My face heated when they kept glancing from him to me, then back again, over and over. *Is it so hard to believe I'm with him?* Apparently so.

Alek had come behind the counter to give me a kiss. Normally, I would have shied away from public displays of affection at work, fearing it looked a little unprofessional, but the way they were visually raping him, I thought it necessary to stake my claim.

He would act in the same manner toward me.

When he tried to back away, I latched on to his shoulders and pulled him in, drawing out our heated hello. My tongue teased his bottom lip, but I stopped before we took it to another plane.

It was easy for us to lose ourselves in one another, sometimes forgetting other people were around.

Breaking free, I shot him a casual look as if I didn't just try to accost him with my desire.

Touching his lips, he furrowed his brow but recovered quickly as he took two steps back.

"Who will we see later?" I asked, not wanting him to ask me about my greeting.

"What?" He looked confused.

"The phone. Who were you talking to? Who are we seeing later?" I repeated.

"Kael. He wanted to know if we were free tonight. I assumed you were, so I said yes. Is that okay? You don't have any other plans, right?"

Those women were still paying way too much attention to Alek, and it was starting to seriously annoy me. I had to remain professional, but I wanted to put them in their place, as well.

With narrowed eyes and an annoyed look on my face, I spoke up, "Can I help you, ladies? Is there anything you're looking for in particular?"

One of the women was really brazen, answering with, "I'll take one of him, please."

Alek busted out laughing but quickly stopped when he saw the look on my face. He ducked his head and fake-coughed to cover up his outburst.

"Well, he's taken. Sorry. Is there anything else I can help you with?"

Her friend had the decency to look somewhat embarrassed, pulling her from the store. "We'll be back later, thank you."

As soon as the door closed, I whipped my head toward Alek. "Did you enjoy yourself, sweetheart?" I mocked.

"You have to admit it was kind of comical."

"I won't admit any such thing. You know damn well if it was a man saying such things in reference to me, he would have been knocked out." He was smiling at me, finding my irritation rather amusing. "Tell me I'm wrong, Alek."

"No, you're not wrong. But it's not the same thing. She was only harmlessly flirting."

"My anger and jealousy is the same as yours." I tried not to let his casualness over the whole situation anger me further. "So there is no difference."

Deciding I wasn't going to ruin my day, or any time spent with Alek, I turned away and took a deep breath, forcing the aggravation from my body. Most of it, at least.

I knew he was standing behind me before he even touched me. He gave me a minute more before he stepped closer and gripped my hips, pulling me back so I was flush with his large frame. His warm breath caressed my neck, then he kissed the sensitive spot right below my ear. He knew exactly what to do to calm me down.

"So...are you free tonight to go out with Kael and Adara?"

Oh, yeah, he did ask me that before my mini episode.

"Yes, of course. I would love to. What time?" I asked, leafing through the invoices scattered on the table. It'd only been three weeks since we'd last seen them but it felt much longer, so I was happy we were going to spend some time with them.

"I'll find out and call you a little later on." Turning me around so I was facing him, he said, "I'm sorry about before. I have to remember you feel jealousy the same as me. But don't ever forget you're it for me. Only you." Then with a quick kiss, he made his way toward the door.

~26~

Sara

The evening couldn't have gone any better. Adara and Kael were a true pleasure to be around. I was becoming fast friends with both of them.

After dinner, we decided to hit a local night club to do some dancing and hopefully burn off some of the decadent calories we had just consumed. It was mine and Adara's take on it, at least. The guys couldn't care less.

Of course, there was no waiting in the long line which stretched halfway down the block. The doorman waved to Alek and gestured us all in immediately. We heard grumblings from the waiting patrons but nothing too bad. There was a part of me that felt guilty we side-stepped all of those other people, but not enough to give it more than a second's thought.

Once inside, we quickly made our way to the VIP section, sat down and ordered our drinks from the waitress who seemed to have appeared out of nowhere. She was quite a looker with her short skirt and too-tight shirt which had *the girls* on display for everyone to see. But I was sure it was done on purpose, working for tips and everything. I glanced at Adara, and we rolled our eyes and laughed. We knew we were being petty, but we didn't care.

"What are you ladies laughing at?" Kael humorously asked.

"The blatant display of goodies," Adara fussed back at him. Her husband scrunched his brow in a questioning look, turning toward Alek to see if he was any the wiser to his wife's comment. He wasn't. Kael shook his head, leaned closer and gave his wife the sweetest kiss.

The waitress returned in record time, no doubt knowing who she was serving, and passed out our drinks. I had to give it to her; even though she almost stumbled over her words when she was talking to both Kael and Alek, she recovered quite quickly. She also had the decency and respect enough not to eye-fuck our men. She smiled almost as sweetly at both Adara and me, probably to exemplify she knew we were with them.

There would be no more questioning thoughts about the poor woman. She had earned our respect, realizing she was there to do a job and nothing more. That, coupled with the fact neither one of our men bestowed upon her a second glance, was all we needed to clinch the fact we wouldn't be feeling the familiar pangs of jealousy where she was concerned.

Toward other women...that was a much different story.

At one particular point in the evening, some random chick sidled up to Alek on his way back from the men's room. She reached up and clutched his upper arm, trying to stop him and pull him closer to her. We all saw the whole scene unfold in front of us. Cautiously, both of them peered over at me, trying to see my reaction. I was doing my best to control my brewing anger, but the drinks I'd consumed were surely stoking that fire.

When the woman wasn't successful in slowing him down, she practically jumped in front of him to stop him dead in his tracks. When he finally did, so as not to trip over her, she took advantage of the opportunity and tried to wrap her hands around his neck. She was blatantly trying to pull him in for a kiss.

Before I could do or say anything, Kael jumped up from his seat and darted over to where his friend was being accosted. As soon as he approached, he gave the woman a disgusted look and saved his dear friend, pushing him out of the way and back toward our table.

Adara spoke up, probably to help distract me from what I'd just witnessed. "Unfortunately, you have to get used to it, Sara. It's part of being with a sexy-as-hell man." She gave me an empathic look, trying to squash any ill feelings I was having at the moment.

"How do you deal with it? Your husband falls right in the same category." *I hope she doesn't mind me saying so.*

She thought for a second before responding. "I'm still trying to figure it out. Even though they play off our reactions as 'cute jealousy', that's not what it feels like. But let some guy talk to us, or

God forbid even touch us even in the slightest way, and they would go postal, raging all around, looking to put someone in the ground."

When I laughed, she looked really solemn for a second.

"Seriously, a few times, I thought Kael was going to be arrested for his actions. Some of the men he went after deserved it because they were being disrespectful, but there were some innocent bystanders, as well. But he's working on it."

"Yeah? How's it going?"

"He's a work in progress." She laughed.

As soon as Alek approached, he felt as if he should explain.

He slid into the seat next to me, leaned close and placed a kiss on my temple. "Sorry about that, sweetheart. I tried to move away from her as soon as I saw her coming my way, but she was a persistent one." He chuckled at the end of his statement, to which I glared in his direction, showing him my disapproval. He stopped immediately, darted his eyes toward the floor and whispered, "Sorry." I shook my head and smirked, allowing him to witness I wasn't as upset as I'd let on.

"Listen, I can't be held responsible for my actions if that skank tries anything with you again. You may be bailing me out of jail tonight." Shrugging, I finished with, "Just saying."

Apparently, my statement was enough to cause all three of them to laugh, which was exactly the type of mood change we needed.

After another half hour of chatting, Adara and I decided we wanted to dance. The drinks I'd consumed loosened me enough to have the courage to give in to the beat. As we were about to leave the table, Alek circled his fingers around my wrist and pulled back so fast I fell into his lap. The kiss he bestowed on me was downright dangerous.

"Be good," he warned.

"I'll behave myself." I stood, grabbed Adara's hand and walked away, but not before I shouted, "As much as I can," over my shoulder. The look on his face was priceless, as if I'd actually gotten one over on him. But I didn't.

I heard him shout, "I'll be watching you," before we disappeared from his line of sight.

"I'm sure he'll be out here soon enough," she yelled next to my ear. "Actually, both of them will be. What the hell am I talking about? There's no way they'll leave us out here alone for long."

"I don't know if Alek even dances. Does Kael?" I had to admit I was more than a little curious as to whether or not Alek would succumb to the thrum of the music. I couldn't picture it, but at the same time it wouldn't completely shock me, either.

"Yes, he'll break out his moves every once in a blue moon." Adara looked quite dreamy as she uttered her next proclamation. "He has quite the moves, on the dance floor as well as in the bedroom." She winked and pulled me into a free area on the dance floor.

I was still laughing when we let the beat of the music take over. There was something about the mix of alcohol, the song playing and the fact all the people around us were strangers, which made the perfect environment to let loose and simply have fun.

When the third song queued up, I was jerked backward until I hit a solid mass of muscle. A quick look of alarm paralyzed my features before I'd realized who snatched me. His scent weaved through the air, calming me immediately.

Alek spun me out before pulling me back close. When his body pressed against my own, I could clearly feel he was aroused, his excitement hitting me in the stomach. "Have I told you how beautiful you look tonight?" he asked as he continued to entice me with his expert dance moves. The way he was grinding on me was enough of an indication I knew exactly what he would rather be doing. Leaning in, he nuzzled my neck, licking and biting my hyper-sensitive skin.

"Why no, you haven't," I lied. He had, but I couldn't help myself; my ego needed a little extra adoration. I knew I was being petty, but whenever there were other women around, especially when they were gawking at him, I loved the extra attention he gave me. I chalked it up to being a woman.

Placing his soft lips over mine, his tongue came out to play, caressing my mouth and asking for permission to enter. Of course, I complied. I wanted to taste him as much as I wanted him to ravage me, but he broke the kiss as quickly as he tempted me.

"You are the most beautiful woman in the world, Sara. Tonight. Tomorrow. Ten years from now."

"Only ten years," I teased.

"Forever." His words relaxed my needy self.

My thoughts drifted to a different version of myself. I'd been the one who was so quick to dismiss any advances someone paid me, shying away from almost everyone in order to protect myself. After what had happened to me, I'd put up a stone wall. Scratch that. I'd put up a concrete tower, surrounded by a moat and fierce, fire-breathing dragons.

No one was going to trick me again.

But somehow, Alek had broken through. I wouldn't call him my knight in shining armor because let's face it, our story was not your typical fairy tale, far from it. But he was able to break down all my defenses and show me a new way of life.

I was different with him.

He protected me, made me feel safe. Admittedly, the way he'd gone about it in the beginning was odd, to say the least, but over time, I'd come to understand his incessant need to follow through on his promise to my grandmother. Especially after he told me what happened to his sister.

I was so caught up in my own thoughts I hadn't even notice Kael and Adara were no longer next to us. Alek and I danced to another song before making our way off the dance floor and back to our private VIP section.

Kael was the only one sitting in our designated area. "Where did Adara go?" I asked, reaching for the last of my drink. I'd worn my hair down, which was clearly a mistake. Gathering the long strands, I pulled them away from my neck, welcoming the shot of cool air which danced over my skin.

"She went to the ladies room. She should be back any minute. Are you guys ready to head out soon?" Kael wasn't tired; I could tell simply by looking at him. No, he wanted to take his wife home and do exactly what I wanted to do with Alek.

"How about one more drink before we go?" Alek asked, already taking a step toward the bar.

"You know I can't refuse you, man. Yeah, what the hell. One more drink to end the night. None of us are driving, so it can't hurt." His eyes lurked around the room, desperately trying to catch a glimpse of his woman.

"Sara, do you want another one?"

"Yes, please," I shouted before he disappeared into the crowd.

I sat down next to his good friend to wait for the return of our significant others. I had never been alone with Kael before, mainly because there was never a situation which called for it. I wasn't uncomfortable or anything...it was just new. I was aware Alek trusted him wholeheartedly; otherwise, he would have never left me alone with him. Either way, Alek trusted at least one other male around me. It was small progress, although, he was coming around to the idea of Matt, as well. I'd seen it whenever I mentioned his name or talked to him on the phone. Alek didn't flinch as much or make any of the numerous scrunched, aggravated faces he used to.

"Sara, I have to tell you. I've known that man practically my whole life, and I have never seen him act the way he does when he's with you. He seems like a different person."

"Is that a good thing?" I asked tentatively.

He hesitated for a minute and my heart hit my stomach. Why was he stalling to answer my question? Before I could have a full-on attack of nerves, he spoke up.

"Yes, it's a good thing. Sorry, I didn't mean to hesitate. It's just...he's never talked about anyone as much or as often as he talks about you. I can tell he's truly smitten, and after getting to know you some, I can definitely see why." He smiled, doing his best to make me feel relaxed after almost freaking me out.

"So, why *did* you hesitate?"

"While I've never seen him so happy, I've also never seen him so wound up and intense before, either. He's constantly worried about you, worried some other guy is going to try and swoop in and steal you from him. It really bothers him. A lot."

So Alek is a little insecure, as well? Good to know I'm not on this island by myself.

"I've never seen him act jealous before, either. Out of the two of us, he was the one who was always so laid-back, letting things roll off him. Even when Cora cheated on him, he just brushed it off, dumped her and moved on with his life. I swear he never looked back. But with you...it's completely different." Kael took a quick breath before continuing. "So yes, it's a good thing. But go easy on my man and try not to give him a heart attack too early."

He chuckled lightly at his own joke and I would have joined him' however, I was too caught up by the mention of some Cora person I'd never heard of before.

Deliberating whether or not I should ask, I deemed I couldn't hold my tongue for one more second. I knew if I waited and asked Alek, he would either not want to talk about it or brush off the question with a general answer. No, if I wanted some info, I had to pry it from his unknowing participant of a friend.

"Who's Cora?" My question was short and sweet.

Kael blurted out the answer quicker than he could even think to falter, probably because he was taken completely by surprise.

"Cora was Alek's ex-fiancée."

My breath caught in my lungs, suffocating me as my brain tried to compute the reality of his words.

Ex-fiancée? Is this really happening? More secrets?

Right after the statement left his mouth, he looked instantly regretful. His next question was gaged solely from my facial expression, which was one of utter shock. "He didn't tell you about her yet, did he?" he mumbled hesitantly.

"Nope." I had nothing left to say.

~27~

Sara

Kael leaned his head back against the seat, puffed out his cheeks and blew out a breath of air. He knew his mistake was going to make his friend angry but in reality, he didn't do anything wrong. Alek was the guilty culprit for not telling me something so crucial. What was he thinking? How could he not tell me he was engaged before? I had so many questions, but I knew I needed some time to calm down before approaching him. I tried my best to take some much needed deep breaths, willing the oxygen to soothe my rising anger.

It was at that precise moment Alek and Adara chose to return to our area. They were all smiles and having a good time. Little did he know the atmosphere would soon change.

As soon as they were close to the table, Kael stood, walked quickly toward his wife and grabbed her by the waist. Leaning over, he whispered in Alek's ear, slapped him on the back and whisked Adara away before she could even say goodnight.

Alek hesitated for the briefest of moments before approaching me.

He knew he was in for it.

A barrage of emotions ran through me, anger and embarrassment being the main two. As soon as he sat next to me, I stood, snatched my drink from his lying hands and gulped it down in mere seconds, the liquor feeding the numbness which had slowly started to wrap itself around me.

When I was finished, I slammed it down on the table and started to walk away without saying a damn word.

But I didn't get far. He reached out and halted me in my tracks with a strong grip around my wrist.

"Take your hands off me, Alek. Now!" I yelled. I didn't have to worry about causing a scene because the only person who could remotely hear me was the man standing in front of me, the guilty party.

Realizing he should give me some space, he released his hold and allowed me to walk away, although he followed closely behind.

Once we were outside I practically ran down the sidewalk, away from him and all his omissions.

"Sara, where are you going? The car is over here."

I whipped around so fast I almost tripped over my feet. "If you think for one second I'm going anywhere with you, you're out of your mind. I'll find my own way home."

How am I going to get home? I didn't think too far ahead.

Seeing how utterly upset I was, he briskly walked past me until he blocked any route of escape. Every time I tried to move, he would shift right along with me, preventing me from going anywhere. I tried to side-step him one more time before I finally gave up, standing there and brewing in my anger.

Alek looked as if he was trying to choose his words carefully, not wanting to dance over the issue anymore. "I know you know about Cora."

Seriously? Out of all the words in the English language, those are the ones he comes up with? How about, "I'm so sorry I lied to you?" Or better yet, "I give you permission to smack me?"

As the moments dragged on, my face became red, my irritation brewing with each breath I took. "Uh...yeah. Kael told me nonchalantly during our conversation. *Why?* Because he naturally assumed you would have revealed something so important to me. How wrong we both were," I huffed.

Daringly, he took a step closer.

"Let's go back to my house, and I'll tell you anything you want to know." I knew I needed time to process all of the information, but I had a sinking feeling he wasn't going to leave me alone until I agreed to go and hear what he had to say.

After what seemed like forever of us arguing back and forth, I relented and agreed to allow him to tell me his side of the story. While

I dreaded hearing of another woman who had come so close to becoming Mrs. Alek Devera, I just wanted the evening to finally end.

As I sat in the passenger seat of his car, I was already heartbroken and he hadn't told me a thing yet.

The entire car ride back to my apartment was spent in silence. I'd told him the only way I would relent and go with him was if he took me home. There was no way in hell I was going to be tricked into going to his house. Knowing it was going to take some time to digest whatever story he fed me, I didn't want to be stuck in his environment. I would much rather he tell me at my place; that way, his ass could leave when he was done.

Once inside, I made a quick sweep of the place to see if Alexa was home. Thankfully, she wasn't.

I had to admit, the ride home squelched some of the initial shock and anger swirling around inside me. Don't get me wrong, I was still beyond words, but I was calming down a little.

I headed toward the kitchen to see if we had anything to drink. Laying off the alcohol would have been a good idea, but I wasn't going to be rational. I found the one bottle of wine we had left.

"Do you want some?" I asked, holding the bottle in the air so he could see it.

"No, thanks. I don't need any more tonight."

"Suit yourself, but I'm going to partake and only be too happy to do so." I couldn't keep the cut out of my tone, not that I was really trying or anything.

When I finally settled on the couch, he came and took the seat next to me. I would have preferred he sit somewhere else, but I wanted the whole debacle over with so I never said a word.

He took a deep breath before speaking. "I'm so sorry you found out like this. Please believe me when I tell you I was going to talk to you about it, but I never found the right time. I was so thrilled you gave me another chance, then things were going so well between us, I didn't want to ruin it. Plus, it was no big deal." If he hadn't been plucking off invisible lint from his sweater, I wouldn't have even picked up on the fact he was nervous. *As well he should be.*

"No big deal?" I asked, each word becoming louder than the previous one.

He looked down at his lap for a split-second. "Sorry, that's not what I meant to say." Lifting his head, he looked directly into my eyes, trying his best to silently plead with me to...what? Forgive him? Understand?

The silence between us confused me more than when he was doing a shitty job of trying to explain. I heard the second hand on the clock above the couch tick by, taunting me about what my future held. Or didn't hold. It would all depend on how things went.

"Start from the beginning, Alek."

"There really isn't much to tell you. I was with Cora for three years, agreed it was time to take the next step and, well...it's how we became engaged." He sensed I was going to interject, so he blurted, "She was the one who asked me, though, not that it makes any difference. The outcome was the same," he mumbled.

"Don't do that, Alek. Don't play this whole thing off as if it's no big deal, simply breezing over the details. You know you were wrong for not mentioning this to me before now. And the only reason you're even saying anything now is because Kael blurted it out." I fidgeted with the hem of my blue dress, doing my best not to let him see me as anything but angry.

"I don't know what else to say except I'm sorry." He tried to reach for my hand, but I pulled back. If he touched me, I knew I was going to eventually give in, and I had to remain strong.

"Who broke it off?" I held my breath. *Please say you broke up with her.*

"I did."

"Why?"

"Does it matter?" he quipped, reining in his quick burst of anger.

"Yes." I needed to hear him say it.

"Fine. She cheated on me." Why did I feel he wasn't telling me the whole story? I didn't press, however, knowing I could only hear so much about her at one time.

I kept at it with my questions. "How long ago was this?" I did my best to compute a timeframe but really, I had no idea.

"A little over a year ago." he replied.

My mouth fell open in complete shock, yet again. Even though I had no idea of the timeframe, I'd honestly thought it had been longer. But a year? Did he still have feelings for her? What if she decided she wanted him back? Would he want to be with her, realizing maybe he made a mistake? They were engaged...to be married. How do feelings go away from something so serious in such a short amount of time?

Time escaped quickly and I still hadn't said anything in response. I didn't even understand the magnitude of what I was feeling. But I knew I should say something. Anything. "Where is she now?" was the only thing which popped into my head.

But it was fair, seeing as how I wanted to know whether or not I would inadvertently run in to her.

"I'm not quite sure. Last I knew, her firm moved her to Paris to head up the division over there. She's an interior decorator, if you were wondering."

I gave him a disgruntled look. "No, I wasn't wondering." *Yes, I am.*

"Sorry. I didn't know how much you wanted to know about her." *That was fair.*

"Alek, be completely truthful with me, because I really need to know. Do you still have feelings for her? I can handle anything if you're honest with me." Keeping my eyes lined up with his was hard to do because all I wanted to do was look away.

He reached over and grabbed my hand. I didn't pull away. "Sara, please believe me when I tell you I don't have any feelings whatsoever toward her. The moment I found out she was unfaithful, I cut her off, emotionally and physically. To be honest, I don't even know if I ever truly loved her. I know it was only just over a year ago since it ended, but for me, it really does feel like a lifetime ago."

There was still something which wasn't sitting right with me. "In all of my searches on you, nothing ever came back you were engaged. Everything else was out there for me to see but not that. Why?"

"You Googled me?" he asked with a lilt to his tone. My statement amused him. His smile tried to break the tension between us. It worked. A little.

"Yes, I did. I wasn't about to go into this blind, although, all the good that did me."

"Please don't say such things." He ran his fingers through his already messed-up hair, deciding what to say next which would appease and assure me.

"You couldn't find anything about the engagement because we never made it public knowledge. I told Cora if I agreed to marry her, then it had to be kept quiet because I didn't want any more of my private life in the public eye. She agreed. Looking back, it should've been a sure sign right there it was a mistake. If I really loved her, I should have wanted to shout it from the rooftops. But I didn't."

His statement pleased me, as much as it could have given the circumstances.

"Is there anything else you want to know?"

Thinking carefully, I chose my next words. "Do you have any hidden wives or children somewhere in the world I should know about?"

Although he was trying to lighten the conversation moments prior, his features locked up tight, proving just how serious he'd become. "No, I don't."

With a suspicious eye, I asked, "Are you sure?"

Because of the half-cocked look on my face, he relaxed a little. "Yes, I'm positive. The only wife and mother of my children I want is you."

Not even possessing the mental strength to deal with such a comment, I decided I'd had enough for one evening. The only thoughts I allowed to consume me were those of climbing into my bed and escaping into the arms of a hopefully blissful sleep. Although, chances of that happening were slim to none.

"Alek, I'm really tired. If you don't mind, I'm going to bed."

"Okay then. Let's go to bed." He rose from the couch and moved toward the hallway.

What the hell?

"Um, excuse me. Where do you think you're going? Don't you think you should be going home now? I didn't say you could stay here." The man was great at testing my nerves.

He turned around briefly to let me know what he thought. "I'm not leaving you. I refuse to go anywhere when you're still so vulnerable. I'm truly sorry for not mentioning that part of my life before, but I don't want to put any distance between us now, physically or emotionally. And I know if I leave you here alone tonight, you'll only stew in your anger and confusion and whatever else you're feeling, and simply put...it isn't good for our relationship. Plus, if you want to ask me any more questions, I'll be right here to answer them for you."

In all justification, I couldn't argue with his reasoning for staying because not-so-deep-down, I knew he was right, about everything. So without further words, I locked up, turned off the lights, and preceded him to my room.

He was thoughtful enough to restrain himself. The only touching which came from him was when he wrapped his arms around me to pull me close as I fell into a restless sleep.

~28~

Alek

I cannot believe shit went down like that last night. What the fuck? While I'd been upset with Kael for telling Sara about Cora the way he did, my anger quickly dissipated. I knew I should've been the one to broach the topic. Should've done it weeks before. But I'd been afraid she would run, fearing I still had a closet full of skeletons, waiting to burst open and topple all over her.

There was only one other thing I hadn't told her, but it wasn't relevant to our relationship. It had nothing at all to do with her, so I chose to keep my mouth shut. Besides, it was too painful to bring up casually.

It was still early, a new pot of coffee brewing in order for me to chase away the rest of my sleep. I knew Sara would be sleeping for a little while yet, so I decided to place a call to my dear friend.

The phone rang five times before he picked up. I smiled at the sound of exhaustion in his voice.

"What the fuck, Alek, it's five in the morning."

"Yeah, well, rise and shine." I allowed some time to pass before I spoke again. "Listen, I just want to tell you everything is, or will be, fine with Sara. While I was pissed you said something, I don't blame you. Not at all. It was clearly my fault for not telling her earlier."

"Well, I'm glad I don't have to worry about you punching me the next time you see me." He chuckled.

"Don't get ahead of yourself. I never said there wasn't going to be payback." I was only half-kidding, of course.

"Yeah, yeah. Hey, did you tell her the full story of what happened?"

Grabbing the back of my neck and squeezing, I tried to rid the rising tension in my muscles at the mere mention of the situation. "No, I didn't. There's no reason for me to delve into it, Kael. What's done is done. Nothing I can do to change it."

"I guess you're right."

"Plus, I don't want to bring up that bitch's name ever again. I'll never forgive her for what she did. Ever."

"Yeah, it was beyond fucked-up, man. I'm sorry you're even having to think about it right now."

"Thanks," I said, rounding the island to grab a fresh cup of coffee. "Listen, go back to bed. I'll talk to you later."

After I hung up, I brought the mug to my lips. As I turned around, the sight of Sara standing in the hallway startled me, causing drops of coffee to hit my bare chest. I jumped back and swore.

"Jesus Christ!" I exclaimed. "You scared the shit out of me." Running a towel over me to clean up, I asked, "What are you doing awake?" *How long was she standing there?*

"I was on my way to the bathroom when I heard you talking to someone." She walked further into the living room. "Who were you talking to?"

Without hesitation, I answered, "Kael. I wanted to let him know I wasn't upset with him."

"At five in the morning? He might be the one who's upset with you now." She snickered.

Maybe she didn't hear as much as I thought.

"Yeah, well, it was the least I could do." Turning back around, I reached for a fresh cup. As I was closing the cabinet door, she asked me a question I knew was going to upset the morning.

"What else happened between you and Cora?" I heard her move even closer, awareness heavily pulsating through me. "I couldn't help but overhear you. Why do you hate her so much? If you never truly loved her, why would you still be upset over her cheating on you?" The tone in her voice dipped. *She thinks I might still have feelings for that awful woman.*

Is there a way to assure her instead of revealing what really happened? Should I try to avoid the subject all together?

Avoidance. Yeah, I'll go with that.

"Don't, Sara. I don't want to talk about her anymore. Please."

"Alek, you have to be honest with me about everything if this is going to work," she replied, gesturing back and forth between us. "You should be able to tell me anything, no matter if it's unpleasant for either one of us. I want you to trust me enough to want to confide in me."

I walked toward her, trying to bridge the undercurrent of separation which was slowing starting to form. "It's not that I don't trust you or can't confide in you, because I can. I just don't want to taint what we have by talking about *her*. She's in my past, and it's where I want her to remain. Please, don't push this."

She looked away before she asked, "Do you still love her? Please, tell me the truth."

Coaxing her chin up so she could see how serious I was, I answered honestly. "No. The only feeling I have toward her is hate." I tried not to give in to my anger, but it spewed forth quicker than I could even think to stop it.

Sara looked confused, and I didn't blame her. "Then why do you hate her so much?"

"I don't want to talk about it."

"Alek, talk to me. Tell me what she could have done beyond cheating that was so awful you have such disdain in your voice when you speak of her. I don't want you to keep things from me. If you don't want me pulling back from you, then you need to be honest with me, about everything. I don't want to feel as if you're hiding things from me."

What the hell? She kept going and going, each word hitting me with such brutal force.

Finally, I snapped. I tried not to, but I couldn't help it. The memories of that day came back at me full-force. Mixed with Sara pushing me, I let go of my reserve and broke apart. I grabbed her arms and pulled her close, the look of anger on my face taking her by sheer surprise. "Fuck, Sara! You want to know what she did?" I yelled.

"Yes," she whispered, so low I almost didn't hear her. I wasn't physically hurting her, but I could tell I was doing some kind of damage to her emotionally. But I pushed all cares aside in order to tell her what she goaded me into.

"That heartless bitch killed my child!" I shouted. As soon as the words left my mouth, I released her from my grasp, turning around so I didn't have to see her reaction.

"I don't understand."

I whipped back around to stare at her. "What is there to understand? I broke it off with her after I caught her cheating on me, and she killed my unborn child for revenge."

The words alone brought the memory back in full-force. I shuddered at the thought of having to relive those moments.

"But if she cheated on you, how did you know the child was yours?"

Out of all of the questions to come flying from her mouth, I didn't expect her to ask me that one. Although, it was the same question I asked myself when I'd first found out, so I shouldn't have been surprised by her curiosity.

"Once I found out she was unfaithful, she blurted out she was three months along. And since I thought the same thing about the paternity, we had a DNA test done. It came back I was, in fact, the father. I told her I would fully take care of my child, but the relationship between her and me was over, for good. She couldn't deal with it, and the following week she had an abortion."

"Oh, my God, Alek. I'm so sorry. I never would've thought..." She trailed off before finishing her sentence.

My anger picked up a new wave of irritation. "You just *had* to push and push until you got what you wanted. Are you happy now?" I paced in front of her, pulling at the strands of my hair, not quite knowing what to do with myself.

"Am I happy she did that to you? Of course not. Her actions were horrific. But am I happy you told me? Yes. I'm not sorry about that."

There was a resolve to her tone I would have normally been proud of, had my anger not overshadowed it.

Deciding it was best for me to finally leave, I escaped into her bedroom to get dressed. When I was finished, I brushed past her and swiped my wallet and keys from the countertop. I was almost to the door when her hands were on me, tugging my arm back toward her.

I shrugged her off me.

"I can't do this right now. I have to leave before I say something I can't take back." I struggled with leaving her, but I needed some time to cool down.

"Okay, whatever you need."

"*Now* you're agreeable?" Right after the words left my lips, I shook my head and turned the knob on the front door. Before pulling it open, I offered, "I'll talk to you later, Sara."

The door remained open as she watched me walk away. I knew her eyes were on me with every step I took, but thankfully, she didn't try to call me back.

~29~

Sara

Half of the day went by, and I still hadn't heard from Alek. No quick phone call or text. Nothing. I decided I would busy myself with some Netflix selections to pass the time. I was halfway through a horror flick when Alexa came strolling through the door. Looking as if she had been about to cry, I patted the seat next to me, hoping she would tell me what was wrong.

Thankfully, she did. "Are you all right, Lex?"

She threw her bag on the ground and slumped back against the couch. "I don't know. I mean, I know what the problem is, but I'm not sure if I know how to fix it. And if I can't fix it, then I don't know how or if I can stay with him." She stood up and wandered into the kitchen. She was searching for wine and thankfully, I only had one glass the night before. Pouring herself some, she tipped the bottle toward me, silently asking whether or not I wanted some.

"Why not?" I still had my own issues I was dealing with.

Once we had the soothing concoction in our hands and were snugly seated back on the couch, we broached the subjects which were plaguing our ever-busy minds.

We both said, "What's the problem with you?" at the same time. After we were done laughing, I urged her to spill the beans first. *I need something to take my mind off my fight with Alek, and her story just might do the trick.*

"You go first, Lex. What's going on with you? Obviously, it was something to do with Braden, so what happened?" Alexa had started seeing him months earlier and everything was going well, so I was surprised to hear something was amiss.

Without any hesitation, she delved right in to what had happened. I'd met Braden quite a few times and while he always seemed nice, he was also a pretty intense guy. But I had one of those of my own, so I could definitely relate.

They proved to be quite challenging, in more ways than one.

"Well, Braden and I got into an argument earlier because he has to go away on business and he wants me to accompany him. But as much as I would love to go, I can't up and take off work for that long."

"Isn't he the CEO of your company?" I was a bit confused. I mean, it wasn't like her boss wouldn't give her the time off, seeing as how Braden was in charge of the whole place.

"Yes, he is, and it makes it all the more reason why I can't just up and leave whenever he wants me to. I have a job I was hired for, and I don't want to be known as *that* girl. You know, the one who's dating the big boss and therefore can do whatever she likes," she said, waving her hands all around. "No one likes *that* girl. *I* don't like that girl, so I won't become her."

"Okay, yeah, I see what you mean now." She drank the rest of her wine and poured another, surely trying to wash away her aggravation. "Merely out of curiosity, does he want you to come with him to help with work, or simply because he wants to spend some time with you?"

"He said, quote, 'I want you to go with me so I can keep an eye on you,' end quote." Her temper was taking hold again, simply from re-telling the story. The statement didn't sit well with her, and I completely understood. Alexa was as independent and stubborn as I was; therefore, I was able to put myself in her shoes. I would be reacting the same exact way if Alek had pulled that shit with me.

But just so I had the full story, I needed her clarification. While Braden came across intense, he didn't seem like the macho, pig-headed type.

"Why does he want to keep an eye on you? What exactly does he mean? Did you ask him?"

"Of course I asked him and he said he didn't mean it the way I took it." Her voice dipped, almost as if she was trying to imitate him. "But what other way is there to take it? When I pressed him further, he said he only meant he didn't like to be so far away from me. He felt like he couldn't reach me fast enough in case I needed him. What I would *need* him for is beyond me. Never mind the fact he's acting all possessive over me recently. And while I find it flattering sometimes, he's getting a little out of hand with the whole fucking caveman attitude."

Alexa almost choked on her drink because of the unexpected noise I made.

"Sorry." I laughed. "It's just I deal with the same thing from Alek. He hovers over me a little too much sometimes, and it really grates on my nerves. I know he's worried about me, but he goes a bit overboard."

"So, how do you deal with Alek when he acts all crazy?"

"I speak my mind and go on about my business. But I'm going to be honest with you, Lex. Even though I speak my mind, we still end up in arguments over whatever he's acting irrational about. But it's the way he is, and if I want to be with him, which I honestly do, then I have to take him as he is. I'll continue to try to make him to see my side of the situation, and if that doesn't work, I withhold sex." Alexa wasn't used to me talking in such a way, having been a virgin before Alek. "Sadly, it doesn't really work so much, because one touch from him and I'm putty in his hands and we both know it."

I hoped my advice helped her, because honestly, it was all I had to offer in the way of dealing with possessive, domineering and stubborn men.

"Braden makes me so mad sometimes, so much so I want to hurtle toward him and knock some sense into him. Physically. You know me, I'm about as laid-back as they come. I don't let things rile me easily, but he knows what buttons to push and he does it quite often." She leaned her head back against the couch and sighed. It was as if she was releasing fifty pounds of stress.

I often mirrored her frustration, more than I liked to admit.

I wanted to make sure of something before I continued with our conversation, though. The answer could alter everything. "Let me ask you this, Lex. Do you ever feel as if he would be physically or mentally abusive toward you?"

Thankfully, there was no hesitation when she answered me. "No, never. He always makes me feel like the most beautiful woman in the world. He's forever praising me and constantly tells me how lucky he is to have found me." She sighed again. "He's just a bit much to handle at times." Shrugging, she stood up. "I think I need another glass of wine. You want more?"

"Sure, why the hell not?" I was going to need a bit more if I was going to delve into my own current situation with Alek.

"Oh, and another thing..." She wasn't done yet. "...if he doesn't lay off about my clothing, I'm going to deck him."

"Why, what does he say?" I knew even before she uttered the words what Braden probably said about her wardrobe. Lex had a revealing taste in clothing. When she was at work, she chose fully appropriate attire, but otherwise, look out. She had a beautiful body and loved to show it off. It wasn't my style, but to each their own. My only concern for her was that sometimes she might attract the wrong attention.

"He says he would prefer clothing which didn't show off all my assets to every man in the world. I tell him I'll continue to dress however I want, which then leads into another heated argument. He always ends the conversations with, 'Well, if I attack someone who's leering at your tits or ass because your clothes are too tight, don't blame me for my *caveman* actions.'" Crossing her arms over her chest was indicative to how she must react in front of him, trying to stand her ground.

I half-smirked before I gave her my opinion, yet again. "Lex, while I don't have the same taste in clothing as you do, I wouldn't change anything. He started dating you knowing you liked to dress a certain way. Why all of a sudden is he having an issue? Let him react however he wants, but your wardrobe is something I wouldn't compromise on. Dress how you want." She looked at me funny and I knew why. "Are you surprised by my reaction?"

"Uh...yeah, a little bit."

"Lex, you're my best friend. What type of friend, or woman for that matter, would I be if I told you to change the way you dressed because some guy has a problem with it? He should count himself lucky you don't wear hot pants and a tube top just to spite him." I laughed.

"Yeah, that would show him for sure." She tapped her finger against her lips. "I do thoroughly enjoy our make-up sex. Hmmm..."

she contemplated. She took another sip from her glass before turning her attention fully on me and my problems.

"All right, all right. Enough about me, you look like you have something you want to talk about, as well. Spill it, sister." I didn't do well with hiding my emotions from Alexa. She could read me like an open book.

"Alek and I had our own argument earlier today, and I'm not sure what to do. I know I have to give him some time to calm down, I just hope he doesn't take too long before he calls me. I would hate to think I pushed him too far. It wasn't my intention. I merely wanted him to open up."

I told her the whole story, from when Kael accidentally let it slip about Cora to what Alek told me about the abortion for revenge.

"Wow, Sara. That's heavy. But you did the right thing. All you were doing was letting him know he shouldn't feel as if he had to keep things from you simply because he felt they were unpleasant."

"It just sucks, you know?"

"Uh, yeah, I do know." She laughed.

Not wanting to talk anymore about my dilemma, I switched it back to her again. "So, how did you leave it with Braden? About you going away with him on his business trip?"

"I told him it wasn't a good idea right now and if he didn't like it, well, he would simply have to deal with it."

"I'm sure it didn't go over too well with him."

"Nope. It didn't. I told him it would be different if I was more established at work, but he was being stubborn. He only wanted to hear what he wanted to. So when he wasn't relenting, I walked out. He tried to stop me, but I made it into the elevator before he could catch me. I actually wouldn't be surprised if he showed up here."

As if on cue, the doorbell rang. We stopped short and looked at each other with the 'it couldn't be' look. What were the chances? Well, with a man like Braden and a woman like Alexa to contend with, the chances were turning out to be very good.

Sure enough, when I checked the peephole, Braden was looming in the hallway. He was wearing his all-too-familiar intense gaze and was pacing back and forth, waiting for someone to answer the door. The doorbell rang again, quickly followed by him banging on the door, calling out for Alexa.

"What do you want me to do, Lex? I'll send him away if you want, but if you want my opinion, you should deal with the situation and talk it through with him."

"Is that what you would do if Alek was out there pounding on the door?" She knew my answer before I said it.

"Yes, I honestly would. It does no one any good to dwell on things and let them stay bottled up." It was how I truly felt.

I gave my friend one last look before opening the front door.

I was taken back by the man's looks. I forgot what a handsome specimen he was.

"Hi, Sara. Can I please come in and speak with Alexa?" Braden was trying to sound calm, but I could tell all he wanted to do was bust through the door and deal with his stubborn woman.

Backing away, I gestured for him to enter. Once he was inside, I gave Alexa a wink and headed for my bedroom so they could have some privacy.

I must have fallen asleep because when I got up to use the bathroom, I heard them making up in her room. I hurried up with what I had to do and ran back to my room, closing the door to try and muffle the sounds.

Honestly, all it did was make me miss Alek even more.

I hoped the next day would bring about a resolution for us. With a heavy heart, I drifted off to sleep, welcoming the passing minutes which would bring me closer to a new day.

~30~

Sara

There was still no communication from Alek. With a somber mood, I made my way toward the bathroom to take a shower and prepare for my day.

I wasn't the least bit thrilled I had allowed a man to weave his way deep into the recesses of my being. I didn't like the feeling of the constant want that was forever plaguing my every thought. I prided myself on being independent to a fault, which also included my emotional state. But the more the weeks ticked by, and the more time I spent with Alek, the less control I had over my emotions.

I came to the quick conclusion there wasn't a damn thing I could do about it. Not anymore.

I arrived to work early to start organizing my day. I was happy to have any distraction; even the most mundane task was welcome. Matt arrived an hour after I did. He looked a bit down, and I wondered if it had anything to do with his friend who he'd been hanging around with lately.

"Matt, you okay?" I asked, filing away some of the older invoices.

"Yeah, I'm fine. Just tired, I think." He tried to pull off aloof but failed miserably. I knew when there was something weighing on his mind, and I was going to try and be the friend he needed.

I reached out to touch his arm, halting his escape into the back room. "Matt, you know if there's something bothering you, you can talk to me, right?"

"Yeah, I know, Sara, and I appreciate it more than you know. I'm not really ready to open up about it right now. But rest assured, when I am, you'll be the first person I go to." He tried his best at a genuine smile before proceeding toward the back of the shop. It seemed he needed a distraction as well.

It was just past three in the afternoon when the bell over the front door sounded. I was busy helping a customer when I heard a familiar voice. Looking up, I came face to face with Cameron, Alek's cousin.

What the hell is he doing here? This is all I need.

It took me some time to even comprehend it was actually him. How did he know where I worked? Was it merely a coincidence?

Something in my gut told me no.

"What are you doing here?" I nervously asked. Oh, God, if Alek walked in and saw him, all hell would break loose.

"Nice to see you, too, Sara." He quickly smiled then looked around the shop, diverting his attention, probably rethinking his ambushing me at work.

"Sorry. You were just the last person I expected to see. What can I do for you?" I was seriously hoping he was there to buy flowers, but the more he stood there, biding his time, the more I knew he wanted something from me.

Cameron kept his gaze on me, glancing from my eyes to my lips, then back again. There was something in his stare which unnerved me. He was calculating, but not enough for me to be fully alarmed.

Yet.

"I was wondering if you were free for lunch. There's a great little café over on Culver Street that serves the best sandwiches." When he sensed I was going to decline, he brought out the big guns. "Sara, I need to talk to you about Alek. You obviously know we're not the closest, but I'm still worried about him and I wanted to run my concerns by you. You know, to see if they're even valid. I need your opinion. I'll only take up a short amount of your time, and then I'll never bother you again." He held up his hand in a boy scout-like salute. "I promise."

I knew it was a bad idea, but if Alek was in trouble, in any way, I wanted to help.

After much hesitation on my part, I gave in. "Fine, meet me there in five minutes."

"Great, see you soon," he responded as he left the shop.

~~~~

I wasn't even paying attention to my surroundings, focused solely on getting our meeting over and done with as soon as possible. The entire situation made me uncomfortable, as if I was betraying Alek on some level.

I saw Cameron as soon as I walked into the café. He was seated in the back corner. He stood as I approached the table, waiting for me to sit before he took his seat again. At least he was being gentlemanly. His actions helped to put me at ease, for the time being.

What I failed to take notice of back at the shop or even at the benefit when I'd first met him was his demeanor. While he portrayed a man of class and sophistication, there was something darker hidden underneath. He camouflaged it well with his smile and charm, his impeccable designer suit and hair styled just so. But his true nature wouldn't be tamed for long. While he was attractive, turning many heads I was sure, he was not to be trusted.

Maybe I was being a little paranoid because I felt so guilty meeting with him, knowing full well Alek would be furious. Trying to push all rationale aside, I sat in silence and waited for Cameron to start talking.

"Thank you for coming, Sara. I really appreciate it." He smiled, and I almost forgot I should be on guard with him. *Yeah, that killer smile sure does run in the family.* But it didn't turn my insides to jelly like Alek's did. Not even close.

Cutting right to the point, I asked, "What did you want to talk to me about, Cameron? What was so pressing you couldn't tell me in person five minutes ago?" I was anxiously awaiting his response but instead of answering me, all he did was smirk, subtly licking his lips. It wasn't until he sensed my discomfort did he start talking.

"Did my dear cousin ever tell you why there's tension between us?"

Okay, where is this going? Was he really concerned for Alek, or was it only a ploy to see me? But why? He knew I was with Alek and I would never betray him. Or did he think he had a shot? I became more uncomfortable as the clock ticked forward.

"No, he never said why. What does that have to do with why you wanted to meet with me?"

He ignored my question, dismissing it as if it wasn't even relevant. "Let me tell you why he and I don't care for each other." Without missing a beat, he launched right into it. "He stole my girlfriend right out from underneath me." He inched his fingers forward on the table and before I knew what was happening, he snatched my hand and pulled me toward him. I was so shocked, I didn't even react. It was as if my brain couldn't comprehend what was unfolding in front of me, like I was in some sort of twisted daze. "And now...I'm going to do the same thing to him."

I mustered up enough force to dislodge his grasp on me. All of my senses came flooding in like a tidal wave. I stood from the table so quickly my chair slid out from behind me and fell over.

"What are you talking about? There is no way in hell I would ever cheat on Alek, especially with the likes of you." His attractiveness faded instantly, and what was left behind wasn't pretty.

As I was about to bolt from the café, he stopped me in my tracks. "Sara, I thought you might feel that way. But it's okay. All I needed was for him to know we met on the sly. It's enough of a seed planted to do damage as it unfolds over time. I simply wanted him to have doubts. The rest will play out just like I want it to."

"Yeah, well, I'm sorry to disappoint you, but I'll never tell him this little meeting took place. And if you try and say otherwise, you won't win. Who do you think he'll believe? Your sorry ass or his beloved girlfriend?"

He kicked back in his chair and folded his arms over his chest. "Sorry to burst your bubble, sweetheart, but he probably already knows." He winked at me and that smug freaking smile crept up on his face again.

I whirled around, searching to see if, in fact, Alek was there with us, but after a quick survey of the patrons, I realized he wasn't.

Sensing my confusion, Cameron pointed out the window, toward a black sedan parked across the street. When I didn't say anything, he filled in the missing piece of the puzzle.

"See the car over there? It's surely one of Alek's minions, keeping a close tab on you. You see, I checked around and found out you apparently have my cousin all twisted up. He is seemingly protective of you, so I don't doubt he's having you watched." The bastard licked his lips. "You know, just in case."

All I wanted to do was smack that look off his face. He continued speaking, although his voice was the last thing I wanted to hear, my mind whirling at the information he spit at me. "I wouldn't be surprised if your phone starts ringing in the next minute or so."

Please, don't ring. Please, don't ring.

Sure enough, thirty seconds later, my phone lit up and Alek's name was splayed across my screen. It had never seemed so looming before. I sent it straight to voicemail, needing a minute to think before I answered. Maybe he didn't know anything and was merely calling me between meetings.

Either way, I needed time to recoup.

Glaring at Cameron, I was determined to get some answers. "Why are you doing this to me? What did I ever do to you? I was nothing but nice to you when we met. I don't deserve this." I had to control my emotions before they got the better of me and I broke down right in front of the asshole. Not because I was hurt but because I was so angry. I wouldn't give him the satisfaction.

"Don't take it personally, sweetheart. You're simply a pawn in an ongoing family feud."

That was his whole reasoning? He didn't care how he used me to get to Alek; the simple fact he was able to use me at all was his goal. How stupid I was to believe he was really concerned about his cousin. I should have heeded Alek's warning when he told me the man was no good.

"Don't ever contact me again, or I'll call the police and slap harassment charges on you so fast your head will spin." I ran out of the café and quickly headed back to Full Bloom.

I was in mid-stride when my phone lit up again.

It was Alek. Again. I still needed more time before I answered, realizing, if he really did know, I'd be in a world of shit. Our relationship was already being tested, and I didn't need to add any fuel to the fire.

In the midst of my phone ringing, a question weighed heavy on me. Was the sedan across the street from the café really someone working for Alek? If so, why in the hell was he having someone follow me?

I won't know anything unless I answer the phone.

Before I could even make a decision on what to do, a car screeched to a halt right next to me.

~31~

Alek

I didn't know what was worse. The fact Sara went behind my back when I specifically warned her to stay away from Cameron, or the fact he had the fucking balls to approach my woman. Again.

To say I was angry was an understatement. I'd calmed down from our previous argument and was going to call her after my afternoon meeting let out. I could never stay upset with her for long, especially since our whole fight started because of me and my failure to tell her about Cora.

But then Brian called me with some interesting information. I'd hired the man to keep a close watch on Cameron, knowing he would try some slick shit like that. I just didn't know it'd be so soon.

I flung open the driver's side door then slammed it so hard I thought the glass was going to shatter into a million pieces.

"Sara! What the hell?" I shouted, walking quickly toward her. I must have given her quite the shock because her hand was still splayed over her heart.

I was next to her instantly, looming over her and pushing into her personal space. She appeared as if she was on the brink of crying, but after a few deep breaths, she tried her best to appear unaffected. As if she had done nothing wrong.

The more silence stretched between us, the more upset I was becoming. *Is she going to try and lie to me? She has to know I know. Why else would I be so upset?*

"Are you going to answer me, Sara? What the hell are you up to? What were you thinking?" My fists curled at my sides, the need to bash my cousin's face in almost too much.

With a calm, controlled voice, she finally spoke. Placing her hand on my arm, she said, "Alek, can we please not do this in the middle of the—"

I cut her off before she finished her sentence. "You don't want to do this in the middle of the goddamn street? Fine, let's go." I reached for her hand and quickly dragged her to my car, coaxing her into the passenger seat before slamming the door. Inhaling some much needed air, I slowed during the walk around to my side of the car. I had to calm the hell down before I actually scared her. It was the last thing either one of us needed. I would never hurt Sara, not in a million years, but the way I was feeling right then was proving volatile.

Once I was situated, I turned my hot gaze on her. "I told you to stay away from him, and you didn't listen to me. Why? Why did you go see him? Tell me." My tempo rose with each question I asked, her silence only spurring me further. *Why isn't she yelling or at least trying to defend herself? Where is the Sara I know who wouldn't take any of my shit?*

When she still didn't answer me, I lost it, punching the steering wheel and exploding with a string of expletives. My episode lasted a whole five seconds, but it was enough to kick her out of whatever fog she'd been in.

Finally, she answered. "He came by the shop and asked to meet me because he was concerned about you." Her tone was flat when she spoke. It was so unlike her.

"He came into your shop? How did he know where to find you?" My last question was rhetorical. I was sure Cameron had plenty of ways of finding out information. I knew he would try to get to her. He'd been trying to pay me back for years, using the excuse I stole his goddamn girlfriend. Never mind he was just an all-around bastard. "Jesus Christ, Sara! What the hell were you thinking?" I repeated.

"I was thinking he was being truthful when he told me he was concerned about you and wanted to talk." A little bit of the fire came back into her voice when she answered me.

"Well, what did he say? What was the big revelation?" I was continuing to take deep breaths, bringing my rage under a manageable control.

"It turns out all he was doing was trying to pay you back for..." She trailed off.

"For what? For me sleeping with his girlfriend...ten years ago? Is that what he said? Was that his reason?"

"Yes." She looked out the window at the people walking by. Her shoulders were slumped, and I hated she looked so defeated. But she had to take me seriously when I asked her to stay away from certain people.

"Well, did he tell you he already exacted his revenge? Did he tell you he was the one Cora had the affair with? Huh? Did he fucking tell you that, Sara?"

Her face scrunched, knowing she was smack-dab in the middle of our twisted feud. His supposed girlfriend I *stole* had gone out with him for a month. She realized what an ass he was, broke up with him and hooked up with me a week later. I hadn't even known they were together, but there was no explaining that to Cameron. *So here we are now, ten long years later.*

"Yeah, I didn't think so. How about the next time I tell you something, you listen to me. Stop going against me, Sara, or else." I knew my last sentence was the wrong thing to say, but I couldn't stop myself.

Her shoulders squared and her back straightened. She turned toward me and let loose. "Fuck you, Alek. I only met with him because I care about you. I really did believe him when he told me he was concerned. It's not my fault you guys are caught up in some twisted, ongoing vendetta. And by the way, how the hell did you even know I met with him? Did you have someone watching me?"

"No!" I shouted. "I have someone watching *him*, not you. Besides, don't turn this around on me. You're the one clearly in the wrong here."

Taking a deep breath, she exhaled and her whole body deflated, although the tone in her voice remained strong. "Well, I wouldn't want you to be subjected to my presence any further then." She reached for the handle and sternly said, "And don't even think about following me." Before I could speak, she jumped out and slammed her door, walking back toward her shop.

We needed the space apart in order for both of us to calm down, so I turned the engine over and sped away.

~~~~

The rest of my day flew by, meeting after meeting keeping me busy. I was thankful for the distraction, but eventually, I was going to have to call her. Truth was, I didn't want to continue to argue, but she had to know how serious I was. Even though I hadn't really loved Cora, the fact she fucked my cousin was a blow to my ego, and I didn't want Sara anywhere near all that mess.

I acted harshly with her earlier, even though I was justified in my actions. In my own head, at least. Before I even thought about ending the argument, my cell rang.

It was Sara.

"Hello." My greeting was more curt than I'd planned.

"Alek...I'm sorry. I know I should've listened to you when you warned me about your cousin. You were right." She exhaled loudly on the other end. I was sure it wasn't easy for her to do, being the first to reach out. "I don't want to fight anymore."

There was a long pause before I responded. I was making her sweat a little. A dick move, I knew. Little did she know I was two minutes away from calling and apologizing to *her*.

"I'll pick you up at your apartment at six."

"I'll be ready."

"Oh, and Sara? Be ready to make this up to me...all night."

~32~

Alek

The next three weeks flew by. Our relationship was fully back on track and I couldn't have been happier. My days were spent in the boardroom while my nights were spent with Sara underneath me.

Everything was going great until one day, I received the phone call I'd always dreaded.

Ever since I'd promised to watch out for her, I knew one day it would come. I'd just hoped it would have been years down the road.

I wasn't ready to deal with it right then.

But I had no choice.

I had to tell her and make sure everything turned out exactly as I wanted.

Sara and I had plans that evening to spend some time with each other. Too bad I was going to ruin it with bad news. But I'd rather it be me than someone else.

The police.

A stranger.

No, I think she'll take it better coming from me, knowing full well I'll do everything in my power to keep her safe and unharmed.

Arriving at her place, I took a quick look around before coming to the hasty realization there was no way she could stay there any longer. Since Alexa spent the majority of her time with her new boyfriend, Sara was home alone—when she wasn't with me, of course.

Somehow, I had to convince her it was in her best interest to stay with me.

We'd been getting along great, minus a couple small incidents here and there, mostly due to my incessant overbearing ways.

"Sara, why don't you grab an overnight bag."

"What for?" she asked, pulling on a pair of dark jeans. "Are we going somewhere?"

"Well, you are. Sort of." As she buttoned her pants, I snuck up behind her and kissed her neck. In a surprise move, she turned around, caught me off-balance and shoved me so I fell on top of the bed.

Straddling my hips, she ground herself into me, instantly making me hard. Not that it took much where she was concerned.

"So," she said, placing her hands on my chest to steady herself. "Are you taking me somewhere?"

"I thought you could take some time off work and spend it with me at my house."

"Oh. Um...can I take a raincheck? Work's really busy right now. Maybe when things calm down a bit, I can. But right now—"

I cut her off because her argument, or reasoning, or whatever the hell she was trying to do was useless. Pointless, really.

"Sara, listen to me," I pleaded as I grabbed onto her hands to make sure she couldn't move away. "I need you to stay with me. I can't explain right now, but I need for you to listen to me. I need you to not argue with me and just do what I say." She struggled in my hold.

"You're scaring me." She continued to try to break free, but I held steady. "Alek, let me go."

"Promise you'll listen to me and I'll let go."

"Okay," she said, tiny spurts of breath being forced from her lips. As soon as I released her hands, she scrambled to the other side of the bed. "What are you not telling me?"

I wanted—no, I needed—to be as close to her as possible. "Baby, let's grab some of your things, go to my house and I'll explain everything. Try not to panic. I'll take care of you. You'll be safe." I reached out to touch her, but she moved away before I made contact, my poor choice of words doing nothing to soothe her rising nerves, no doubt.

"No, you tell me what's going on right now or I'm not going anywhere." She was so resolute I knew damn well if I didn't give in, I was going to be carrying her out over my shoulder. I was trying to be better with that shit, so I moved to the edge of her bed, preparing to tell her what I'd found out not even an hour before.

Without knowing what else to say, I blurted out the first thing which came to mind. "He's out. I'm not sure what happened yet, but for some reason, they let him go, Sara."

My eyes never left her face. I wanted to remain strong, even though inside I was breaking. I was terrified my world would be ripped apart if anything happened to her.

Taking a deep breath, I pushed all of those damn crazy thoughts aside, knowing I'd do whatever it took to keep her out of harm's way. Some of it she wasn't going to like, even fighting with me over it, but I would never waver. I would never give in, no matter how much of an issue she gave me.

"Who are you talking about, Alek? Who's out?" Her voice was quiet. I saw a flicker of fear pass through her as she hopped off the bed.

"Samuel." It was the only word I uttered, but it was enough.

She sunk to the floor and cried. "No, not now. It can't be." She cried harder. I rushed to her, fell on my knees and pulled her to me. "They told me he'd probably never be released from there. It's only been eight years." She hiccupped, trying her best to catch her breath.

"I won't let anything happen to you, baby. I promise. I have people looking for him. I promise I'll find him."

I think my words made her feel better, if only for a brief moment. "You do?" she asked, gripping onto me for dear life.

"Yes. Of course I do." Helping her to her feet, I asked, "Now, will you come stay with me for a while?"

There was no hesitation on her part. "Yes," she whispered.

After she'd gathered her things, we were on our way toward my house.

Little did she know she'd be staying with me a little longer than I'd originally indicated.

~33~

Sara

It was the following morning as I was preparing for work when Alek sprung yet another surprise on me. While what he'd told me rocked me to my core, I was grateful he was in my life. I knew he would do everything in his power to protect me, more than ever.

He didn't say it, but I saw the fear in his eyes when he was telling me about Samuel. I didn't let on, though. I didn't want him to think I doubted his ability to keep me safe.

Because I didn't.

"Can I help you with something?" I asked as he stood there, shower door wide open, letting in the cool air. His eyes roamed over my body, lingering on my breasts before flicking up toward my face.

It took him a couple seconds to compose himself before he responded. "Since I knew you would've argued with me to no end, causing me unnecessary stress, I've agreed to let you go to work today. However, I've made some specific provisions you'll have to follow."

"You have *allowed* me to go to work?" Why did his words not surprise me? I turned around so I was fully facing him, my hands resting on my hips. I knew he was going to go overboard, so I should have known better.

I didn't think I'd ever become used to his domineering attitude. I thoroughly enjoyed it in the bedroom when we were in the throes of passion, but otherwise, it was downright irritating. Even if I understood where the man was coming from.

"Yes, Sara. I'm allowing you to go out into the world, knowing he's out there somewhere. I won't relax, not one bit, not until I find him and can make sure he never hurts you again. So, as I was saying, I've made some specific provisions for today and going forward, until I deem unnecessary. Since I can't be right by your side every second of the day, I hired security to keep you safe."

"What are you talking about?" I was done with the damn shower. I rinsed the rest of the conditioner from my hair, turned off the water and wrapped a big, fluffy bath towel around myself.

"I'll be driving you to and from work, every day, until I know for sure there is no threat. Then, when I'm not able to be near you, Brian will watch over you. Keep you safe."

"Who the hell is Brian?"

"Aren't you listening to me? I just told you Brian is the man who will be watching over you when I can't." Sarcasm encased his tone, diminished only by the slight smile on his face.

"And where, pray tell, is Brian going to be? Is he going to be glued to my side the whole day? How am I going to explain his presence to the people at work? Huh, Alek? Tell me."

"He'll be camped out in his car, making occasional trips into the shop to verify everything is okay. He has a picture of Samuel, so he knows who to look out for, just in case. And as far as explaining him, that's up to you. Whatever you want to tell people is fine with me."

Knowing I wasn't going to win the battle, I shrugged, shook my head and walked away from him. I grabbed an outfit I'd brought with me, getting ready in record time.

My mood probably had something to do with it.

"Can we please go now?" There was no missing the annoyance in my voice.

"You can be as pissed off at me as you want, Sara." He followed me from the room and down the long hallway leading to the steps. "Oh, and by the way, if you try to leave the shop without him, he's instructed to follow you and call me immediately. So don't get any crazy ideas."

I knew I was being irrational. I should have been grateful he cared as much about me as he did, going the extra mile and hiring someone to watch out for me when he couldn't.

Yet I couldn't help but feel as if it was only the tip of the iceberg. Knowing Alek, he wasn't going to let me breathe unless he or someone else was there to witness it themselves.

~34~

Sara

Weeks passed by, and although I loved playing house with Alek, shacking up in his enormous home, I started to go a bit stir-crazy.

I hadn't gone anywhere without either him or Brian. At first, I was a bit afraid of the man, all six-foot-four-inches of him. He was a wall of hard muscle, with a shaved head and dark, intimidating eyes. The only thing which put me at ease was when he smiled, which wasn't often at all. He was a quiet guy, intent on only doing the job he was hired to do.

I needed a night out with my friends. *Only* my friends. When I talked to Alek about it, he flat-out refused. Mentioning Matt would be there with us didn't anger him as it used to, which I found both odd yet refreshing. But he still told me no. *Maybe next time.*

Both my good friends knew what was going on with me. Alexa had known the entire time, of course, but I'd had to fill Matt in right after Alek told me about Samuel being released from the institution. Once Matt had gotten over the initial shock of it all, he looked about ready to kill. He became almost as unbearable as Alek, ensuring I wasn't making any more deliveries by myself, even threatening to call Alek if I gave him a hard time.

Damn those men for wanting to look out for me. I knew I was blessed, truly I did, but they were just too much sometimes.

I was in the middle of filling out an order form when Alexa called.

"Hey, girl, what's up?" I asked, leaning back against the counter, taking extra time to focus on my conversation.

"Since I haven't seen much of you lately, do you want to grab a drink after work tonight? That is if Alek will let you out." She chuckled.

Not funny.

Initially, I felt bad leaving Alexa in the apartment all by herself, but the reality was she spent half the time shacked up with Braden anyway.

"I would love to. I really need to go out. You know, hang out with my girl." A bit of tension fell away as I looked forward to the night ahead. "There's no way I'm going to be able to ditch my bodyguard, so I'll be picking you up. Or should I say *we* will?"

"What? Alek's not going to be glued to your hip?" she asked, as I heard her muffle a laugh.

"Nope. He's tied up in business meetings until late this evening. He already told me."

"Okay, then I'll see you later."

I phoned Alek an hour later to let him know of my plans. He wasn't happy about it, but once I pleaded my case, he came around. Well, enough to let the issue go, knowing Brian would be there to watch over me.

One of the other conditions was we had to go to Throttle. He said he would feel better not being with me if he had multiple sets of eyes on me, his security at the club being the other babysitters for the evening.

I feigned inconvenience, but in reality I didn't mind. We loved the place, although that was going to remain my little secret.

Walking into the club, I realized people were staring. I was sure it had something to do with the giant walking too close behind us. We were drawing attention and I told him as much, ushering him to the far corner where he could still keep tabs on us but be out of the way of prying eyes.

"Lex, I'm sorry I had to bring Brian, but you know everything that's going on." I took another sip of my drink and waited for her to respond.

"Don't apologize, Sara. I totally understand. At least he's easy on the eyes." She laughed as she glanced in his direction. "Speaking of hot men, how is the gorgeous devil himself? How are you two getting along these days?"

"Good," I answered as I took another sip. "We have our moments, of course, but overall, I couldn't be happier." Losing myself in thoughts of Alek was quickly becoming my favorite pastime.

I had to force him from my mind, though. That night was about me and Alexa and us partaking in some overdue fun.

As our conversation wound down, a club mix of "Blow" from Ke$ha pumped through the speakers. The beat pushed us to give each other the look, the one which said *let's dance our asses off, baby.*

Dancing until I couldn't feel my feet anymore sounded like just what the doctor ordered. Alexa and I slowly walked toward the bar. We were content with our little area when all of a sudden the bartender asked us if we wanted to step up and *shake it.* With little hesitation on our part, we climbed onto the stools then onto our new stage. It was a bit of a feat since both of us were dressed in skirts, mine a bit shorter than I'd typically wear.

I saw Brian advance in our direction, but I was successful enough in halting him with a simple glance. He retreated toward a nearby corner, keeping his eyes intently on the both of us.

The club was filling up to capacity, making what I was doing all the more daring. Many pairs of eyes were glued to us, watching every move we made. Normally, I would've never done such a thing but after the weeks I'd had, I needed to let loose and not take everything so seriously.

Was it reckless? Maybe.

Was it fun? Abso-fucking-lutely.

We were three songs in when Alexa bumped my hip and pointed across the crowded floor. I had no idea who she was pointing at until I saw him weave through the throngs of people, his angry eyes locked on me as he moved toward the bar.

I should have stopped dancing. I should have gotten down from the bar. I should have made up any excuse I could think of to erase the annoyed look on his face. I didn't want to fight with him, but I didn't do any of those things.

Instead, I kept on dancing.

I made eye contact with him long enough to let him know I saw him, but not long enough to fuel his bad mood any further. He made his way to me within seconds, looking up at me with a familiar scowl on his beautiful face. Grabbing my ankle, he almost made me stumble. I reached for Alexa's arm, which was thankfully near me, and kicked off his hold from my foot.

"Get down! Now!" he yelled over the music. Because I'd been dancing up and down the bar, I made it harder for him to physically latch onto me. I laughed inwardly to myself. I would've thought he'd have taken the hint and backed off. But deep down, I knew better. He wouldn't stop until he accomplished what he'd set out to do, so I continued to enjoy whatever time I had left up there.

We managed to have some fun before Mr. Buzzkill showed up. I wasn't doing anything wrong. It wasn't as if I was stripping my clothes off as I danced. It didn't matter, however, because according to Alek, I was putting myself in some sort of danger.

Speaking of which, where's Brian? Searching the crowd of people, I saw him leaning against the wall, shaking his head in disapproval.

I wonder who called the big boss man?

I came crashing back to reality when someone's hands gripped my waist. Without even noticing, Alek had shoved his way through the crowd of people below us, reached up and grabbed me, jerking me down toward him. A startled scream escaped me, even though I shouldn't have been surprised.

I scrambled to break free once my feet were planted firmly on the ground, but no amount of resistance was allowing me to escape his hold. He gently grabbed my upper arm and practically dragged me away at a hurried pace.

Once we were in a calmer part of the club, he spun me around in front of him and stared at me, still seething. "What did you hope to accomplish with your little show, Sara?"

"I was only dancing. You're the one who always makes it more than it is. You don't ever want me to have any fun." I pouted, stumbling toward him, but I quickly caught myself.

"Are you drunk?"

"No...maybe...yeah, a little bit." I snickered, trying to step back to put some distance between us. He hated when I drank without him, and I wasn't making much of a case for myself in my inebriated state. *Oh, well.*

"I'm taking you home. Now."

"No, you're not. I am *not* leaving Alexa here, plus I'm not done having fun."

"Do you think it'll be fun when some drunk bastard has you pinned against the wall?" He was so dramatic. He had two sets of security watching me. Obviously too close since he was called in to *rescue* me. "We are leaving right now. I'll arrange for Brian to drop her off, anywhere she wants to go."

"Braden won't like that," I muttered, reaching for his shoulder to steady me. The heels I was wearing were probably not the best choice. *Yeah, blame the shoes.*

"Who the hell is Braden?" he asked, a sour tone to his voice.

"Alexa's boyfriend. He's like you," I said as I tapped his cheek three times. "He won't want some strange, cute man dropping off his woman."

I wasn't sure if Alek was upset or amused. His cocked brow was confusing me, and even the slight tilt of his lips wasn't a clear-cut sign. He could've been holding back his anger for fear we would get into another disagreement. Or maybe the four drinks I'd had earlier were messing with my ability to see the situation for what it was.

Alek being Alek.

"So, you think Brian's cute?" he asked, tugging me closer.

"Sure. If you like the 'I could tear you apart with my bare hands' look." The lopsided grin on my face told him I wasn't the one who took notice of the man's looks. Although, as my best friend had mentioned earlier, he *was* easy on the eyes. Placing my lips over his, I muffled, "Alexa said he was cute, not me." I didn't want him to think I was gawking after my security detail.

He planted a quick kiss on my mouth before ushering me toward the front door. When I realized we were leaving, I stopped dead in my tracks, Alek slamming into the back of me.

"Jesus, Sara. What are you doing?" He tried to walk around me, linking his fingers with mine to pull me forward, but I didn't move.

"No, I can't leave her," I repeated.

"I told you she'll have a ride home."

"No," I repeated stubbornly. Crossing my arms over my chest, I leaned against the nearest wall, my lips pursed in annoyance.

Frustration poured off him as he stood his ground. Moving two steps closer, he placed his hands on my waist. "What do you want me to do? Do you want me to take her with us? Do you want me to have her call Broden?"

"Braden," I corrected.

"Braden, Broden, who the hell cares? Do you want me to have her call him?"

"Can you go get her, please?" I was all over the place and was sure I was becoming quite the pain in the ass. All he was trying to do was take me home, yet I was obstinate at every turn.

But that's what he gets for interrupting girls' night.

Blowing out a deep breath, he actually went in search of my best friend. "Stay here," he warned before he walked away from me. Knowing he wouldn't leave me totally alone, I caught Brian propped against a table, not twenty feet from where I was standing.

Two minutes later, Alexa walked toward me with Alek in tow.

"Are you leaving, Sara?" she asked, but she already knew the answer to her question.

"Mr. Grumpy Pants wants to take me home." I laughed. Alek shook his head behind Alexa, obviously finding my state of ill-repair a tad comical. *At least he's not flying off the handle and shouting out some of his crazy demands.* Latching on to her hand, I pulled her in close so I could whisper in her ear. Or at least I thought I was whispering. "Do you want cute Brian to take you home, or are you going to call sexy Braden?"

"I can hear you," Alek shouted. The look on his face made me laugh.

Not sure what was going to transpire, Alexa pulled out her cell phone and dialed her boyfriend's number. She walked away while putting a finger in her ear, trying her best to block out some of the noise of the club. After only a minute, she hung up and headed back our way, grinning so big I knew her man was on his way.

Alek summoned Brian over with a simple wave of his hand.

"What do you need?" he asked, his eyes solely on the man who employed him to be there that evening.

"Stay here and make sure Alexa is picked up. Blend in with the crowd around you, though. I don't want to cause any issues between her and this Braden guy." Turning his head in my direction, he said, "Satisfied? Cute Brian is going to wait here until sexy Braden picks up your friend."

I couldn't help it. I busted out laughing. The way Alek mocked my earlier words was too much to contain a straight face.

He nodded toward Brian, indicating we were leaving. Alexa and I hugged, but it wasn't quick enough because before I knew it, Alek had slapped me on the ass. I yelped.

"Let's go," he demanded impatiently.

Without further delay, he led us outside.

~35~

Alek

I seriously didn't know what I was going to do with her. She drove me crazy sometimes but in all reality, I wouldn't change a damn thing.

Sara wasn't obliterated, not even close, but she was definitely feeling relaxed. I hated she'd gone out without me, but I knew she was going stir-crazy holed up in my house. Fearing Samuel would somehow find her weighed heavy on her mind, as it did mine. So I'd relented and allowed her to go out with Alexa, with the stipulation that Brian accompanied them.

And what happened? He called me to tell me she was dancing on top of the bar, like she didn't have a care in the world. It was too risky, so I hopped in my car and drove like a mad man to Throttle, only to catch her in mid-gyration, dancing her ass off to the beat of the music.

While I'd instantly become excited, as had every other fucker watching her, I couldn't have her on display like that any longer, so I forced her down. I knew she thought I was ruining her fun, but I'd be damned if any other man was going to eye-fuck my woman.

I tried my best to rein in my temper, and I thought I'd done a pretty good job. Taking into account everything she was going through and stressing about, I totally understood her wanting to be free for a night and have a good time.

But enough was enough.

"What are you wearing?" I asked, placing my hand on her bare thigh. We were en route home, but I couldn't stop myself from at least inquiring about her clothing choice.

"Clothes."

"Very funny. Where did you find that outfit? I know it's not yours."

"How do you know? I could have gone shopping. You don't know," she mumbled as she looked out the window.

Inching my fingers until they rested on either side of her knee cap, I gripped her skin and clamped down. She twitched her leg and laughed, trying to pry my hand off her.

"Stop."

"Tell me where you got the clothes," I teased, preparing to grip her knee again.

"Okay, okay. I'll tell you. Just don't do it again." She was smiling widely, and it was the most beautiful sight. "They're Alexa's."

"I figured as much. Don't you think they're a bit too small for you?"

"Did you just call me fat?"

"What?" I exclaimed, totally taken off-guard. "No, of course not. All I was saying was...you don't...you shouldn't be wearing her clothes. You know, because you're bigger than she is." Slapping my hand on my forehead, I knew she'd just managed to fluster me.

"You *did* just call me fat," she cried, trying to push my hand from her leg.

"That's not what I meant at all. I meant you're taller than her. You're not fat," I said, turning my head to look at her. And what did I see? Her...smiling. She was messing with me, and I fell right into her trap. "Nice going. You're going to pay for that one."

"Promises. Promises," she teased.

Once we arrived home, I made my way toward the den to grab a quick drink. I knew I needed to rid myself of the residual anger which was swirling around inside me. She was safe. Sara was home, and I could relax.

All in all, I think I did well. I normally would have screamed and shouted, but I held my tongue, instead giving in to the situation and finding humor where I could.

It was damn hard, but I did it.

"Alek, I'm going to bed now," she proclaimed, making her way toward the staircase. I hated the clothes she had on, but I loved to watch the sway of her hips in that damn skirt.

"Wait up, I'll come with you." I threw back the remainder of my drink and placed the glass on the table, doing my best to hurry the hell up.

"Oh, no, you won't. You're sleeping somewhere else tonight, mister."

My steps faltered. *Is she upset with me?* "What are you talking about?" I asked, approaching the bottom step. She was halfway up the stairs, completely ignoring me. "Sara," I called out. "Answer me." I took the steps two at a time, but she was already down the hall and rounding the corner of the bedroom. Before I could catch up with her, she disappeared from sight, closing the massive door behind her.

I reached forward, my fingers circling around the large handle. I tried to turn it, but it wouldn't budge.

Did she just lock me out?

"Sara!" I roared. "Open the damn door." My heartbeat picked up pace, a light sheen of perspiration breaking out along my forehead. I hated when I couldn't reach her, being locked out of the bedroom no exception. "Open up!" I shouted, pounding my fist against the grain of the wood.

"Forget about it. I'm not unlocking the door. You ruined my one night out in weeks and as punishment, you can't sleep in here. With me." I heard her fumbling around then I heard a loud crash. "Shit!" she yelled.

What the hell? "Are you all right? What happened? Sara, open the fucking door."

Silence.

For some of the longest seconds of my life.

Then her voice carried through the air. "I'm fine. But you've got to forget about the bedside light. It's gone to Lamp Heaven." She laughed.

I was glad someone thought the situation was funny.

There was no way I was going to allow her to lock me out of my own damn bedroom. Not without valid reason, and cutting short her girls' night because she was being inappropriate sure wasn't one. The side of my fist hit the door again and again, but still she didn't let me in.

What the hell is she doing in there?

"Open the goddamn door! Now!"

"You can forget it, so just go sleep in one of the other bedrooms, Alek. And calm down before you give yourself a heart attack."

"You're going to be the cause of my heart attack, *sweetheart*. I'm giving you one last chance. Open this door now before I break it down." *Yeah, I took it there, and I'm completely serious.*

"You wouldn't."

"I'll do it, I swear to God. You have five seconds. One. Two. Three. Four. Five."

Bang! Bang!

All of the adrenaline coursing through my veins had become too much to bear. I grabbed hold of the sides of the frame and prepared myself to kick in the door. I'd never done anything like that before, but they made it look easy in the movies. How hard could it be? Looking at the size of the door, I almost changed my mind. I didn't want to break my damn foot. But deciding I indeed had to reach her, I reared back and gave it my best shot.

It didn't budge, but I saw the wood splinter around the edges. Making sure I was at a better angle, I pushed away from the frame again and with every last bit of energy I possessed, I let loose.

It worked.

The massive door toppled to the ground inside the bedroom.

The look on her face was priceless. She was shocked I'd followed through with my threat. *She shouldn't be, though, knowing I'm indeed a man of my word.*

"I told you to open it, Sara. See what happens when you don't listen to me?" My chest rose and fell rather quickly, my shirt clinging to my skin. I'd surely exerted enough energy, but I was still raring to go.

Stepping over the broken wood, I slowly made my way toward her. She'd taken off her clothes and was standing before me in nothing but her bra and panties, hands resting on her delicious hips as she tried her best to glower at me. Who did she think she was kidding? I saw her eyes light up with desire as soon as she saw me.

"Now what?" she asked, faux aggravation distorting her lovely features. "What did your little spectacle accomplish? Tell me."

"Nothing will ever keep me from you, Sara. Nothing," I declared. My words were the God's honest truth.

My stride was unaffected as I crushed the small distance between us with only a few paces. Looking as if she was contemplating escaping, I reached out to grab for her, but she jumped on top of the bed. She made her best attempt to flee on the other side but I caught her in midair, flipping her around and tossing her on her back.

Time to check if our little dance turned her on.

~36~

Sara

Alek pinned me to the bed with his strong, forceful body. I couldn't move, not an inch. His thighs pushed my legs apart as he grabbed my wrists and pulled my arms above my head, holding me in place.

"Why do you provoke me so much, Sara? Do you love this side of me?" He pushed his thick erection against me, grinding his hips as he spoke.

He didn't even wait for me to answer him before he claimed my mouth, rough and possessive at first. When I didn't resist, he softened his kiss and devoured me with such passion I thought I would explode right then and there.

Freeing my wrists, I lowered my arms so I could feel him, grasping on to him to try and pull him even closer.

"Do you want me to fuck you?" His tongue played over the skin of my throat. "Are you wet for me?" he asked as his hand disappeared down the front of my panties. Running his fingers through my swollen folds, he found his answer. "You are. Did our little cat and mouse game make you hot?" he whispered against my ear, nipping the sensitive skin as I bucked beneath him.

"No," I lied.

"I hate when you don't tell me the truth, sweetheart. Don't you know I'll have to punish you now?" His lips drove me insane, his tantalizing tongue bringing every ounce of lust directly to the surface. *As if that's hard to do.*

"Okay," I whispered into the crook of his neck.

"Okay, what?" he goaded, loving every bit of his power over me. He was going to make me say it, except I wasn't going to dance around anymore.

"Punish me. Give it your best shot."

A low groan escaped his throat as he snatched my wrists back up and held them above my head. "Be a good girl and make sure you don't move, no matter how much you want to." His bottom lip disappeared between his teeth as he set about binding my hands with soft sashes he'd pulled from underneath his bed.

"Were you hiding these?" I asked, wriggling my arms.

"Simply had them handy in case I needed them." He winked before making sure my other arm was also secured.

Straddling my waist, he pushed up my lace bra, freeing my heavy breasts for his enjoyment. "Do you want me to kiss you?" he asked, pinching my nipples until they were painfully erect.

"Please," I begged, his touch the sweetest torture. I didn't want him to stop, but I wanted him to finish me off all the same. Do me in before it became too much.

"I love that your body belongs only to me." He lowered his head until his mouth hovered above mine. "Mine forever," he whispered. His tongue slid along my lower lip, teasing and tormenting me so badly I almost screamed in frustration. But he never fully kissed me.

Is this part of his punishment?

Swiftly moving his way down my body, he captured a breast in his mouth, the sensation of his lips pushing me toward the edge. As his teeth softly grazed my nipple, my back arched off the bed, a guttural moan filling the air between us.

"Do you like that?"

There were no words, and thankfully, he didn't make me answer because I'd become too lost to waste my energy on mere syllables.

Finally, he moved lower. Without a single sound, he gripped the sides of my unsuspecting panties and ripped them away from my body in one fluid motion.

"Sorry." *No, he isn't, and neither am I.* "They looked expensive," he said, kissing the flat of my belly. "I'll be sure to replace them."

"Why? So you can rip those, too?"

He never answered, instead spreading my legs and pushing them toward my chest. At first, I found the position strange, but when his mouth covered my slick heat, I discovered it might be my new favorite.

"Alek," I cried out. "I can't...please, let me go." I pleaded with him to untie my hands so I could have more control, but he shook his head as his tongue lavished me with his dark need. He never used his hand on me, his mouth the only weapon of choice.

The stubble from his jaw added to the sweet torment. "Are you close?"

I could only nod, my teeth capturing my bottom lip to keep from screaming.

"Really close?" I looked down at the man torturing me and locked eyes with him. I nodded again, my breathing picking up pace the more my body crested toward release.

"Good." He pulled back instantly, moving off the bed and away from me.

"What are you doing? Where are you going?" He'd reduced me to nothing but a mess of desire and was loving every single second of it.

He never answered me, instead slowly discarding his clothes. Once he was bare, he climbed back on top of me. Moving his hands toward my wrists, I'd thought he was going to free me, but instead, he tightened the material binding my hands.

"What are you doing?"

"You sure are full of questions, aren't you?" He gave me a kiss before placing his hands on my waist and flipping me over. On my stomach, my arms formed an X above me. It was slightly uncomfortable, but I wasn't in any pain.

When I started to speak again, he slapped my ass, quickly shutting me up. "Don't think, Sara. Just feel. Close your eyes and give in to your body's needs." He moved my legs apart again and placed his hand underneath, covering my throbbing core. His finger found my clit instantly. At first, it was slow then the more my body reacted, the quicker his ministrations became.

But again, he pulled back once I was ready to tip over the edge.

No amount of begging or pleading was going to make him give in.

This is his punishment for locking him out.

After more excruciating minutes of pleasure and frustration, he lined himself at my entrance and was about to thrust into me when my words echoed around the massive room.

"Don't even think about it. Not without a condom."

I didn't have to look at him to know he was disappointed. We had to have a talk about his sudden need to knock me up. I'd told him my feelings on the subject, yet he still tried to get one over on me, thinking my incessant need to come would outweigh my reasoning.

"Are you sure?"

"Yes," I affirmed.

"Fine." Grumbling, he reached into the bedside drawer and retrieved the barrier I'd insisted he wear. When he was ready, he positioned me on my knees and thrust forward in one fluid motion.

He stretched me in the most delicious way, making no qualms about doing his best to derive his own pleasure.

"Fuck, Alek...I can't...hold back." My words escaped me as he pushed into me over and over again. My pleasure was building, threatening to toss me over the cliff frighteningly soon. I'd never exploded so quick before, but I wasn't complaining.

"Tell me when you're going to come," he grunted, his own pleasure surely beckoning him to fall, as well.

"Why? So you can stop?" I clutched the binds and held on for dear life. It was starting to happen, but I wasn't going to say a word to him. I desperately needed my release.

He leaned forward and bit my shoulder, his tongue sweeping over the affected area to soothe the sting of pain. "I don't need you to tell me, sweetheart. I can read your body better than you." He licked the shell of my ear. "You're so close." He thrust deep. "Too close."

Before I could argue with him, he retreated, the absence of his body causing me to cry out in frustration. But I knew better than to ask questions or argue with him. He was going to do what he wanted and there was no changing his mind.

Untying my wrists, he spoke softly. "I'll allow you to come. But it's going to be while you're facing me. Watching you unravel is my new favorite thing." He kissed my cheek as he finished unknotting the material. When he was done, he flipped me back over but instead of lying on top, he sat with his legs wide, leaned back and pulled me onto his lap. Before I even realized what he was doing, he'd impaled me onto his thick cock. I screamed, the bite of pain no match for the pleasure he coaxed from me. He rested on one hand, his other circled around my waist to keep me steady.

Looking into my eyes with overflowing lust and desire was enough in itself to be my undoing but he had other plans for me.

"Ride me, baby. I'm letting you take the reins this time." Releasing any kind of control was new for him. So as to not waste the gift he'd given me, I took full advantage.

Rotating my hips had him coming undone at the seams. But it was nothing compared to my next move. Slowly, I pushed myself up from his lap, allowing him to slide from my body until only the tip remained. Then I gently lowered myself back down, swiveling my hips again once I'd reached the base of him.

There was nothing sexier than making Alek moan in pleasure. It was a major turn-on for sure. The most animalistic sounds erupted when he was in the throes of passion.

His sounds were *my* new favorite thing.

"Fuck...you feel amazing. Yeah...keep doing that." His head fell back, fully content with my slow assault. His sexy throat was exposed and all I wanted to do was lick his salty skin. So I did. I ran my tongue all over him. He flinched when I hit a sensitive spot.

His hand caressed my back as I coaxed his pleasure from him, satisfied with our painfully slow dance.

Until he wasn't.

Without warning, he pushed me until my back hit the bed, threw my legs over his shoulders and pounded into me as if he'd lost all control. Our new position allowed him to go deep, making me scream out his name with every thrust.

"I can tell you're close, but don't come without me." He captured my mouth, nipping at my lip before our tongues swirled together, tasting and demanding more from each other.

"Alek...I can't...I can't wait." My cries were desperate. I wanted to wait for him, but unless he was right there with me, I would be detonating around him soon.

His ragged breaths and quick, muffled moans were his telltale signs he was ready to go over.

"Hold on, baby. Just a few more seconds." Lowering my legs, he urged me to wrap them around his waist. His body moving inside of mine was the best feeling in the world.

He owned me.

Every part.

Seconds later, he released himself, calling out my name as his pleasure became too much.

And I was right there with him.

Countless minutes passed before either one of us was able to regulate our breathing. Once the initial bliss had faded, Alek escaped into the bathroom, returning a minute later with a warm washcloth. "Spread your legs," he teased.

"Again? Boy, you can't get enough of me can you?"

"No, I can't. However, this time, I simply want to clean you up. Now, spread 'em."

Of course I did what he asked, widening my thighs so he could run the cloth over my sensitive skin. Every touch he bestowed upon me was like Heaven, his after-sex ritual no exception.

After he disposed of the material, he crawled back into bed, pulling me to him so he could cuddle with me. Placing his hand on my waist, he pushed himself against me as he kissed my neck.

I decided it was time to address the elephant in the room. "You know the door is not a simple fix. You busted the hell out of the frame when you couldn't control yourself." A half-smile lifted my lips.

"I don't give a shit about the door. I'll have it replaced before tomorrow evening. Just don't make it a habit of making me break them down." He nuzzled closer, his warm breath tickling my ear. "I'll break down every barrier you have just to reach you. I need to get to you, without fail."

There was a desperation in his voice which was hard to hear. I wasn't going anywhere. I wanted to shout it from the rooftops, but only time would prove to him I was his. Always.

I wished there was a way I could make him understand exactly how much I loved being with him. I always felt safe when he was near me. Hell, I knew I was safe out in the world just knowing he was watching out for me. *Ironic, isn't it?* The same thought which made me smile caused me to run away from him initially.

I loved the way he had the power to turn me on with a simple smile. I loved the fascination which overwhelmed me when he was near. Even when he was acting jealous and throwing his weight around, I loved to engage him in every way possible. I loved every single aspect of his complicated personality.

I loved...

Him.

I love him.

What the hell am I waiting for? He'd expressed his feelings for me before, but he stopped, not wanting to rush or have me return his affections simply because *he* had.

But I loved him, and it was time he knew.

Turning to face him, I gently stroked his jaw as I prepared to say the three words I knew he wanted to hear. Three words I couldn't believe I hadn't said before.

I parted my mouth to speak and a soft sound escaped his lips. His eyes were closed and his breathing was slow.

He was asleep.

Another time then.

~37~

Alek

I would never tire of waking up next to Sara. I couldn't believe my luck; she'd chosen to be with me, especially after everything that happened. But she'd forgiven me and we'd moved on.

As always, one look at her and I was fisting myself, ready to claim her and make her scream out my name. Her body was draped over mine. Her leg grazed against my most sensitive area, and I was praying to God she didn't jerk around in her sleep. Her long, dark hair fanned all around her, enticing me to twirl it around my fingers. I pictured pulling on it as I was fucking her from behind, anchoring her to me so the only escape she had was when I pushed her toward her orgasm. All of the ways I could defile her filled my head, feeling a little guilty when I looked at her sleeping form again. She looked like an angel.

Too bad. I wanted to be the devil right then.

"Are you going to stare at me all day?" she mumbled, opening one eye so she could look at me. The sweetest smile danced across her lips, and my heart skipped a beat.

"I would if I could."

She rolled over onto her back and stretched, pushing her glorious tits in the air. She wasn't playing fair. One movement and I simply couldn't control myself.

I shifted her quickly so she was beneath me, the look of surprise on her face comical. "Good morning, sweetheart. Do you want to play?"

"Always."

"Good answer." I moved back until I was positioned at her feet. She looked at me strangely until I took her foot and rested it on my shoulder. Nipping and kissing the sensitive area around her ankle made her squirm, but I didn't stop. I continued to move toward her calf, then her knee, finishing off by gently biting her inner thigh. As she moaned her approval, I threw her leg over my shoulder and got into position. Reaching next to me, I grabbed a condom and quickly sheathed myself, rolling my eyes at Sara as she watched me do it. "What?" I asked as she continued to shake her head.

"Nothing. I find it funny you're still waiting for me to give you the thumbs-up to fuck me bare."

My eyes widened at the use of her language. I loved the fact she felt so comfortable with me, her candid words certainly amusing.

When my cock was perfectly aligned with her heat, I stopped. Before I entered her, I looked deep into her eyes, licked my lips and announced, "Mine."

She didn't say anything, choosing instead to arch her back off the bed.

"Mine," I said more brusquely.

"You make it seem as if I'm your *possession* the way you stake your claim."

I knew she was playing with me. The cock of her brow told me so. "Mine," I reiterated. My jaw tensed, my grip on her hip tightening.

"Alek," she lazily chastised. "Do you think I'm one of your possessions?"

"I treat my possessions well. Wanna see?" I smirked, knowing I would obtain the exact answer I wanted, eventually. While it started off as a game, it'd become quite serious. Sara was mine, and I wanted her to acknowledge as much.

I needed to hear her submission.

I lowered my mouth until I came in contact with her throat, sucking lightly so I could mark her.

"Mine."

Next, I flicked my tongue over her lobe, capturing it between my teeth and gently biting down, causing a shudder to rack through her body.

"Mine," I whispered in her ear.

My lips traveled until they met hers. I kissed her. Slowly. I set the pace and she let me. My tongue teased her, twirling around and around, so hungry to taste her.

I briefly broke our kiss. "Mine."

There was nothing left for her to utter except the truth.

"Yes. Yours," she breathlessly replied.

~~~~

Whisking Sara away from Seattle was looking more and more appealing. I had some quick business to attend to in California, and I wanted to take her with me. The initial meeting concerning the restoration of my newest hotel would only take me a day, at most. I'd initially planned on only being away for twenty-four hours, but I'd decided to extend the trip, devoting an additional three days to my woman. We would relax in bed after devouring each other for hours on end, walk on the beach, take in some sight-seeing and whatever else she wanted to do while we were there. I was at her mercy. Whatever she wanted, I would gladly give to her.

I'd already discussed my plans with Matt for the upcoming trip in hopes he would be able to look after Full Bloom while we were away. I knew Sara felt guilty every time she had to ask him to step in and cover for her, mainly when I'd required as much, so I went ahead and made plans behind her back. He was only too willing to help out. He knew all about Samuel and agreed it would be a nice change of pace for her to go away for a few days. She needed it. Hell, we both did.

Surprisingly, I'd come to trust Matt to be my eyes and ears when I couldn't be with Sara. Well, other than Brian, of course. He'd proven to be someone who was genuinely concerned about her well-being, a trait I had to admire. I no longer feared he wanted to sleep with her, his fondness toward her much like that of a brother to a sister.

I tried my best not to show her how worried I was every day we couldn't locate the man who had devastated her world once upon a time. Words of comfort spewed from my lips and they seemed to do the trick most days, but in reality, I was scared shitless he would find her again.

Needless to say, my overbearing ways had intensified ten-fold. If I wasn't with her, then Matt was, and when neither one of us could be, Brian took over. When it became too much, she argued. She gave me the silent treatment. She even cried on occasion. And even though her tears were like tiny shards of glass ripping at my heart, I never wavered.

I couldn't.

She meant more to me than my own life, and I would always protect her.

Even from herself.

~38~

Sara

I was excited about the upcoming weekend. Alek was taking me away to California on one of his business trips. He promised me we could do whatever we wanted. And I was definitely in the mood for some sunshine, ocean and reclusiveness with my man.

I was going to tell him I loved him while we were away. I tried to speak the words before but he'd fallen asleep, and there was no way I was going to say them when he couldn't hear me.

I had loved him for quite a while, and I thought it only fair he be privy to that information. Warmth encased my heart at the thought I was going to open up that part of myself to him. *And I know he'll keep it safe...and protected.*

Alek had informed me all arrangements for my shop had been made. At first, I was a little miffed but the more I thought about it, I viewed it as a win. The simple fact Matt and Alek could talk, let alone make a plan together was huge progress. So I wasn't going to look a gift horse in the mouth. I'd take it and run with it.

I needed to run a last-minute errand, a little lingerie surprise for our getaway. I was able to give Brian the slip, and I was giddy I actually pulled it off. I knew Alek wasn't going to be too happy, but I would be seeing him soon enough. And once he saw the reason for my escape, I was sure he would forgive me instantly.

It was getting late and the sun had officially gone down for the evening. Walking back toward my car, I thought I heard a noise behind me. I turned quickly and found nothing but my overactive imagination.

Relax, Sara. You're working yourself up over nothing. Damn Alek and his constant paranoia to keep me safe.

I clicked the key fob to unlock my doors as I approached the driver's side. The interior light from the car provided me with some sort of relief, the darkness surrounding me a little overwhelming.

As I attempted to open my door, my keys slipped from my fingers and fell to the ground. I was trying to juggle my purse, drink and the packages I'd purchased, and it proved to be too much.

Great. As if I'm not freaked-out enough, I drop my keys. Isn't that exactly what happens in the horror movies? The woman drops her keys, which allows the crazy psycho enough time to grab her?

What the hell, Sara. Stop freaking yourself out. Everything is fine. I had to think of something more pleasant before I got myself too worked up.

I retrieved my fallen keys and opened my door but before I could escape to safety, someone tugged on my arm.

I whipped my head around to see who it was, petrified for a split-second. Until I was met with the familiar sight of Brian.

"Jesus Christ, Brian! You scared the shit out of me. What the hell are you doing?" I didn't mean to sound so harsh but he really did scare me.

"Nice play giving me the slip, Sara. You know Mr. Devera would have my head if he found out. If you value my life at all, you won't do that to me again."

I knew he was right. Alek *would* be pissed at me but more so at him because he trusted him to watch out for me.

I was so wrapped up in my own thoughts and the guilty feelings which washed over me at putting Brian's job in jeopardy, I didn't even see him approaching us.

A static fog enveloped me, freezing me in place. Everything around me moved as if in slow motion.

I saw him coming at us, yet I couldn't do anything.

I couldn't say anything.

I couldn't even warn Brian.

Before my brain could even tell my mouth to move, speak the words which were so obviously caught in my throat, Brian was on the ground and taking me with him. An object crashed down upon his head, pushing him forward and catching my leg in the process. I fell to the ground right beside him

When I looked up, trying to make sense of what just happened, I was met with *those* eyes.

Those vacant, dark, soulless eyes.

His hair was different, longer and unkempt, as if he was trying to hide from everyone in plain sight. The longer I stared at him, the longer time seemed to stop. The only thoughts which flooded my brain were those from so long ago. It was as if nothing else had happened in my life.

No Seattle.

No new friends.

No new job.

No Alek.

I was simply frozen with fear.

"Hi, Sara," he said in the most haunting voice imaginable. He was so calm. Too calm. "I've missed you so much." His head was centered perfectly between his shoulders, but when he asked me his next question, he tilted a bit to the left, almost as if he was daring me to utter the wrong answer. "Have you missed me?"

He advanced toward me, not even waiting for my response.

There was nowhere for me to run. But I had to try. I had to try for myself but more than that, I had to try for Alek.

I stumbled away from him, almost snapping my wrist in the process. When I thought there was enough space to do so, I jumped to my feet, but it was too late. He grabbed my hair and yanked me backward until I hit his chest.

An all-too-familiar sour smell I had long-tried to forget smothered me.

I flailed like a fish out of water, trying to escape his grasp, but all I accomplished was inhaling more of the odor into my lungs, suffocating me with every breath I tried to take.

The world quickly faded around me, the darkness but a heavenly godsend to the reality I was thrown into. At least in the dark, I wouldn't see his face. Or hear his voice. Or feel his touch.

~39~

Alek

I couldn't stop grinning like a fool. I was finally going to have Sara all to myself, alone for the whole weekend. No friends to distract us, no job to get in the way. Well, I had a bit of a distraction but only for a short time, then she would be all mine.

I had half a mind to tie her to the bed and not let her up until we had to head back home. But I knew she was looking forward to spending some time on the beach, so I'd have to share her with the world. For a little while, at least.

Oh, shit! I better check what bathing suit she packed for our getaway. I could only imagine. I'd prepare myself because I knew unless she planned on donning a burlap sack, we were going to have words about what she wanted to wear on the beach.

I decided to grab a quick drink to calm my overactive mind before I started to feel the familiar pangs in my chest. I got so worked-up sometimes it was hard to calm down. Although, I was making an honest effort to do so. For her. And for me, so I didn't keel over from a heart attack.

Loving that woman was the best thing to ever happen to me. But my God, I was petrified all the time something was going to happen to her. I had those feelings beforehand, but ever since I'd lost sight of Samuel, I was even worse.

I loved her strong-willed spirit, and I wouldn't want her to change for anything. But because of the way she was, she also tested the edges of my sanity.

I was nervous about the upcoming weekend. I wanted our relationship to continue to move forward, and I was planning on asking her to move in with me...officially. She was staying with me for the time being only because of the threat of Samuel, but I wanted her to make the decision to *want* to live with me. For good.

I had to make sure my approach was gentle and not stifling at all. If it was, she would back away, and I didn't want that to happen. Shit, if it was up to me, we would've been making plans to be married and working on our first child.

But with Sara being the more rational one out of the two of us, I had to proceed with caution, so as not to overwhelm her.

Glancing down at my watch, I noticed time had escaped me. It was much later than I'd thought. I wondered what kept her. We had plans to catch a late dinner then turn in because of our early trip.

I busied myself in my office, trying my best to allow my work to distract me. Plus, any extra time I could dedicate to Sara was time well spent in my opinion.

I was lost in spreadsheets before I noticed it was well past the time Sara should've been home. Dialing her cell, I fully expected her to pick up, so I remained calm. Until there was no answer after my second attempt.

Then my third.

Then my fourth.

Panic coursed through me. I tried to remain calm and remind myself sometimes her ringer was shut off. Even though I had repeatedly reminded her it was in her best interest to make sure the damn thing was on.

I tried her one more time before letting my anxiety take over. "Come on, baby, answer the phone. Come on," I whispered.

The more time passed the more of a wreck I became. She would never be so late without at least calling me. Somehow, she would find a way to contact me. We weren't fighting, so there was no reason for her to purposely give me the silent treatment.

Right before I totally freaked out, my phone rang. With a loud exhale of pent-up breath, I answered without even looking to see who was calling.

"Hello."

"Hi, this is Maggie from St. Luke's hospital calling."

My heart fell into a black hole. *No. No. No. She can't be hurt. She just can't be.*

The lady on the other end of the phone continued to speak. "Do you know a Mr. Brian Alvarez?"

What? This isn't about Sara?

"Sir? Are you still there?"

"Sorry, yeah, I'm here."

"Do you know a Brian Alvarez? Your number is in his phone."

"Yes, I know him. Is he all right?" I asked in confusion, still trying to process the rapid thoughts, which were scrambling around in my head.

"It seems he was attacked earlier this evening. He's doing better, but he took quite a blow to the head."

I hung up the phone after letting her know I was on my way. I was halfway out the door when it dawned on me Brian was keeping watch over Sara.

So, where is Sara? And who assaulted Brian?

Once I entered his hospital room, I knew it was bad news, not only for Brian since he seemed to be in pretty bad shape, but also for Sara. I had a gut feeling she wasn't simply late coming to the house.

No, something was terribly wrong.

Brian saw me as soon as I walked in and immediately looked anywhere but directly into my eyes.

Yeah, this is bad.

"What happened?" I strode closer to his bedside so he didn't have to turn his head to speak to me.

"Damn it, Mr. Devera. I don't know. One minute, I'm talking to Sara and the next I'm on the ground, fading in and out of consciousness. The only thing I saw was Sara fall down next to me and a shadow of another person looming over her. Then I blacked out for good. Next thing I remember is waking up in this hospital bed."

My mind was reeling. My worst nightmare had come true.

I knew who the shadow was.

It was *him*.

It was Samuel.

I ran.

I ran from Brian's hospital room.

I ran until I reached my car.

I didn't know where I was going but I was going to find her.

I would cease to exist if she was taken from me. I was more alive than I'd ever been since that fateful day I decided to walk into her flower shop and finally meet her in person.

I found exactly what I had been yearning for my entire life.

It was the day I took my first breath.

And I wasn't going to let anyone take her from me.

Not ever.

I needed to find her so I could breathe again.

To be continued in

Wanted...

Coming July 7, 2015

Acknowledgements

Thank you to my husband for being patient with me as I released one book after another, spending countless hours locked away in my office. Thank you for giving me the time I needed to get these characters out of my head and onto paper. I love you!

A huge thank you to my family and friends for your continued love and support. I don't know what I would do without you!

To the ladies at Hot Tree Editing, I can't say enough great things about you. You continue to amaze me and I can't wait until our next project together. You have been truly fantastic!

I would also like to thank Clarise at CT Cover Creations. Your work speaks for itself. I'm absolutely thrilled with this book cover. It's beyond gorgeous!

To Beth and Renee, the feedback you've given me with each story is priceless. Your continued support means more to me than you will ever know!

To all of the bloggers who have shared my work, I'm forever indebted to you. You ladies are simply wonderful!

To all of you who have reached out to me to let me know how much you loved Addicted, and are anxiously biting your nails for this book...here you go. Enjoy!

And last but not least, I would like to thank you, the reader. I hope you enjoy the next installment of Alek and Sara's story.

About the Author

S. Nelson grew up with a love of reading and a very active imagination, never putting pen to paper, or fingers to keyboard until two years ago.

When she isn't engrossed in creating one of the many stories rattling around inside her head, she loves to read and travel as much as she can.

She lives in Pennsylvania with her husband and two dogs, enjoying the ever changing seasons.

If you would like to follow or contact her please do so at the follow:

Email Address: snelsonauthor8@gmail.com

Facebook: https://www.facebook.com/pages/S-Nelson/630474467061217?ref=hl

Goodreads: https://www.goodreads.com/author/show/12897502.S_Nelson

Amazon: http://www.amazon.com/S.-Nelson/e/B00T6RIQIQ/ref=ntt_athr_dp_pel_1

Other books by S. Nelson

Stolen Fate

Redemption

Addicted (Addicted Trilogy, Book 1)

Made in the USA
Middletown, DE
17 January 2018